Line

The Lure of the Mer Book Two

by

Laney Kaye

Line

Contact Information: info@thewildrosepress.com

Cover Art by *Diana Carlile*

The Wild Rose Press, Inc.
PO Box 708
Adams Basin, NY 14410-0708

Visit us at www.thewilderroses.com

Publishing History
First Scarlet Rose Edition, 2019
Print ISBN 978-1-5092-2551-4
Digital ISBN 978-1-5092-2552-1

Published in the United States of America

How can one woman excite him more than two centuries of philandering?

She wound her fingers into his hair but groaned as sand speckled them both. "Ugh. You know what's wrong with sex on the beach?"

"Worst name for a candle fragrance, period?"

"Yeah, well, there is that. But the sand. Sand is not sexy. Grit gets into...well, everything. Total mood killer." Dammit, why was she talking now? Why had she let the sudden rush of nerves, a pathetic concern about being once again owned, spoil the moment?

"Wow. Way to destroy the fantasy of a holiday romance for thousands of people. Hope you're not a copywriter."

She snorted. "Sorry, am I cutting your out-of-hours perks? Someone needs to tell it like it is. Fantasies are the biggest con of all time. They belong with rainbow-pooping unicorns, fairies, and...and"—she jabbed a finger at his mermaid tattoo—"those. We're indoctrinated at birth into believing we have to chase a fairytale to be happy, conditioned to think we need to find Mr. Right, marry, have our two-point-three kids, and then life will be happily-ever-after. And you know what? We're so busy waiting for the mythical fantasy to begin, we forget to live in the now."

The lifeguard withdrew his hand from her shorts and shifted away from her, lying on his side. "Ah. That's a hint you want me to back off."

She clambered to her feet, the move nowhere close to elegant. Darn it, why had she given up yoga? "Not at all. I don't do hints." Not this new version of her, anyway. "It was an invitation to come and get wet with me." She shucked her shorts and kicked them toward her T-shirt.

The lifeguard rose lithely. He probably did yoga. And tai chi. And weights. "Phrased like that, there's no way I'm saying no."

Dedication

As always, for Taylor, who cheerleads
and chastises with equal enthusiasm

Special thanks to my editor, Jo, for repeatedly
handling my dangling modifiers

And with gratitude to my critique
partners—particularly Lindsay, Sandie, Jes, & Marty—
for their unblushing input, support, and expertise

Chapter One

Since his brother deserted him, breaking the law of the Mer by greedily taking a human lover for himself instead of sharing, Erik had been washed up. No sex for over a week, a fact his coral-hard cock pulsed into him in visceral Morse code, leaving him aching with unfulfilled lust.

It wasn't like he couldn't have found a bit of willing pussy—or a number of other accommodating options—but two hundred years of practice had him accustomed to doing his fishing with Trent.

He flicked his hand idly back and forth on the polished abalone-shell bench, watching the webbing between his fingers appear and disappear. For all the action he was getting around here, he may as well have taken a trip to Lesbos. He'd done that once. Pure torture. Not the ten-thousand-mile swim from his offshore home on the tropical Australian coast to his ancestral seat in Greece—as one of the last of the Mer, swimming came as naturally as breathing—but his frustration upon arrival, discovering he'd been cock-blocked by false advertising.

Despite the creation of the island in his great-great-great—to the power of who-could-even-calculate-what now—grandfather's days, as a legendary hot spot for beautiful women conducting a male-oriented sex trade, things had changed. Sure, there were half-dressed, nubile females as far as the eye could see, but they were all searching for the particular type of pleasure popular myth now claimed the island provided. Accordingly, not one had a skerrick of interest in him.

Poseidon was no doubt pissed at the corruption of his corruption.

The driftwood-framed door of woven seagrass slammed back on its hinges, the bang muffled by the leagues of water cocooning their underground lair in the ancient lava tubes that created a subaquatic world known only to the Mer.

Well, known only to the Mer until his brother, Trent, had brought his new human partner home after rescuing her from drowning a week ago.

Trent crossed the cave in a few strides. He bent to root around in the icebox and pulled out a pitcher of milk, waggling the jug at Erik. "Drink?"

Erik snapped his laptop shut. It wasn't like he'd been able to focus on tracing the ownership of the illegal fishing fleet, anyway, despite the urgency of identifying the men who'd assaulted Jayde and tossed her from one of their trawlers. The lack of blood reaching his brain, as it insisted on surging far lower, made any form of concentration unlikely.

The rubber feet on the unit squealed across the counter as he shoved it away and shook his head. "No, bro. Not like *I've* done anything to work up a thirst."

Trent sloshed the contents of the jug. "We're just about out."

"Yeah, well, whose fault is that?"

His brother ran a hand through disheveled blond hair and shot him a shamefaced grin. "Sorry. This pressure to perform solo is all kind of…new. Have to keep my strength up."

"Told you I'd be happy to help you out."

Trent snorted and chugged milk direct from the jug before replying. "And I told you that is *never* happening."

Like all Mer, the last descendants of Poseidon, the brothers could only take a human lover as part of a ménage, to ensure the combined pheromones of two Mer disrupted the involuntary genetic modification mating caused to the human. For more than two centuries, Erik and Trent had shared their women.

Then Trent met Jayde and chose to sacrifice immortality to claim the voluptuous marine biologist for himself.

True love, or some such crap.

Trent splashed milk into a glass, and Erik grunted. Apparently, Jayde needed to keep her strength up, too.

"I'll head topside and pick up some more a bit later," Trent said. He shoved the empty jug back into the icebox Erik had painted with the words *Davy Jones' Locker* decades earlier. A nod to their heritage. "Bring it back for you to turn sour with a look."

Erik ignored the jibe. "What, you reckon you can manage to stay off the nest long enough to do something so mundane and potentially lifesaving as heading ashore to fetch groceries?"

Trent drummed his fingers on the counter, squinting as though he considered the question. "Green's an unattractive color on you, dude. In any case, I figure I'll take Jayde with me. Whole other lot of beds to break in at the apartment."

They kept a townhouse at The Point, a secluded gated community on one of the two cliff-side horns of land protecting a huge bay. A great, golden curve of palm-lined beach separated them from the small town and the lifeguard station they manned on the sun-soaked strip, close to one of the dangerous rips that marred the warm, crystal waters of the Coral Sea. Their neighbors within the complex were wealthy weekend residents who either didn't notice or didn't question the brothers' irregular presence. Or the varied company they kept.

With the exception of Jayde, most women probably wouldn't take too kindly to the labyrinth of undersea caves, remnants of a millennia-old volcano, which were their true home. A more human-friendly version of a residence made for far less explaining—and also meant Erik could indulge one of his other passions.

He snorted. Maybe it'd have to become his only passion, given that it didn't seem he'd be getting laid anytime soon. "If you head in, least I won't have to listen to the two of you." Apparently, Jayde was neither a timid nor quiet lover. And lustful moans were the last thing Erik needed to hear in his newly celibate state.

Trent rooted around in the cupboard as though his waving hands had some chance of making food miraculously appear. Wasn't quite how their Mer abilities worked. "One of us needs to pick up some grub before the meeting, too," he said. Neither of them big on cooking, they preferred to grab a meal at one of the beachside cafes at the end of their shift with the other Mer lifeguards from their squad. "Make it a bit less bachelor pad, a bit more hospitable in here."

"By 'one of us,' I take it you mean me?"

"Just trying to give you something to keep your hands busy, little brother. You can't be beating off all

4

the time." Trent ducked as Erik flipped a ball of seawrack at him. "Yeah, see, that's what I mean. There you go, playing with your balls again."

"Did you—?" Erik broke off, looking toward the tunnel that led to the access chamber from the ocean.

Trent looked in the same direction, alerted by the telepathic communication the Mer shared. He groaned. "Damn. The Pod made good time. Currents must have been in their favor."

"Damn?" Erik lifted an eyebrow. "Some host. The way I recall it, you summoned them."

"Yeah, well, like you said, we need Mer hands on deck to chase down this fleet."

Erik blew out a sharp breath. "I promise you, I never made such a crap joke."

Trent's expression took on the determined look he adopted each time he discussed catching the trawler crew who'd assaulted Jayde. "If the trawlers have headed farther north up The Great Barrier Reef, that's Daniel's domain. Best he hear straight from Jayde what these guys are capable of. Plus, he might know something about that bastard Mer working with them. Not like there's so many of us the Senior Council can't keep track." Trent's hand moved to his shoulder, rubbing at the already-healed gunshot wound from a week earlier when he and Jayde had been apprehended boarding the trawler to seek evidence of illegal fishing activity. "Hey, you didn't tell Dan about Jayde, did you?"

"Nope. I've not talked"—Erik tapped his temple with a finger, referring to the Mer ability to communicate telepathically—"with him for weeks." He shot a grin at his brother. "But as it's such a salacious story, I did broadcast it to all the guys at The School. So I guess Dan could've picked up on it."

"Yeah, whaleshit, mate." Trent snorted. "Add lying to the growing scroll of things you're crap at. Can you imagine, though? Be Mer murmurs by the time it'd been telepathed through twenty lifeguard stations."

He raised his hands defensively. "I swear it started out as 'bro's hooked up with a human' not 'Trent's shagging a siren.' "

"Swap your name for mine, and that wouldn't even be newsworthy, would it?"

"Doesn't matter anymore. I've decided to become a monk." He leaned back on his stool, arms crossed on his chest, legs stretched across the cave.

"More like a sea monkey, I reckon."

He let out a whistle of disgust. "Bro, you need to lay off the sex a bit. Jayde's sucking the humor out of you. Not that you ever were that funny."

Trent rubbed at his jaw. "Yeah, I forget the Uncle Zeus-type jokes all belong to you. Speaking of sucking, can you cover for me for a while?"

"With Jayde?"

"Nice try. You planning to keep that up for the next few decades? Just entertain Dan and the rest of The Pod for a half hour."

"Half an hour? Bro, that's embarrassing. You're really letting the side down." He shoved up from the bench, his bare feet curling over the undulations of the lava-flow floor. "Oh, and, dude? With a houseful of Mer, you might want to tell Jayde to keep it down a bit. At least until you've introduced her to the family, y'know."

Trent rifled a hand through his long blond hair,

blowing out a tense breath, a mixture of embarrassment and pride. "Will do. Just don't mention her to The Pod yet, okay?"

Palm up, Erik headed for the door. "You're all on your own with that one, but I'm taking front row seats. Can't wait to hear you 'fess up how you were willing to trade immortality to fuck a human."

Trent lifted a shoulder, his grin easy. "Not just any human. Only Jayde."

Erik stuck a finger in his mouth and retched. "Whatever, dude. Clock's ticking. You're down to twenty-eight minutes now. Make it memorable, because she knows where to find me."

He headed toward the access chamber as Trent strode in the opposite direction, through the coils of the lava tube tunnels.

The water in the entrance pool swirled, creating a vortex. Knee angled to place a foot on the rocks behind him, Erik leaned back against the wall, watching the inky spiral and focusing his mind on the approaching Mer. Counting them as he registered each individual thought.

Easiest to hear were those closest bonded to him by blood; his uncle Daniel and immediate cousins, Jaxson and Tyson. He straightened in surprise, alert as he felt Elena in his thoughts. Mer men outnumbered the women by about three to one, and Elena would've rated on that basis alone, without the lure of her dark-haired, dark-eyed, island beauty. However, she'd amped up the attraction by proving to be unattainable. Not only had she refused every Mer man who'd tried his luck, there were no rumors of her hooking up with humans, either.

Hell of a waste.

Her record of rejection wouldn't stop him having a crack, though, but he'd have to pick his moment. One "no" was all a Mer required, their code of honor tight when it came to consent. Had to be that way to maintain some kind of discipline, given their voracious sexual appetites.

He kicked from the wall and leaned down to the pool, extending a hand as his uncle surfaced.

Daniel hoisted himself over the rocks surrounding the edge of the pool. Accompanied by the tang of fresh salt, he shook off the droplets that rolled from his naked torso like water from a seabird's feathers, and then clasped Erik's forearm in a strong hand, pulling him close and throwing a well-muscled arm around his shoulders. "Erik. It's been too long."

"Too right, Dan. You're looking good."

Dan had to be hundreds of years old, but like all Mer, he'd reached a point where he'd stopped aging. Or at least, the dude aged so slowly the progression was unnoticeable. Though his features were craggy and weathered, he rocked it like a guy who lived on chia pots and avocado, enjoyed hanging in the surf, and could be found doing yoga on cliff tops as the sun came up. Only his thick silver hair gave any real hint of age.

Erik flicked a hand at the churning water as another swimmer emerged. "I hear you've brought a few of The Pod."

Dan nodded. "Left a few shifts at the base, but brought the boys down early. They're raring for a bit of your southern-style excitement, figured we could spend a couple of days here before the Senior Council meet." He bent to help a blond-haired, younger version of himself out of the pool.

"Jax." Erik fist-bumped his cousin. "Good to see you." Next to Trent, Jaxson was Erik's favorite fishing companion. They liked the same kind of girls, the bubbly, outgoing ones who were up for a good time, not intimidated at the thought of taking on a pair of huge Mer. And above all, not clingy.

"Dude. The old man promised me there'd be a better chance of picking up a bit of tail down in your neck of the woods. It being a tourist Mecca here, and all."

"No promises, but plenty of tourists. Didn't think there'd be shortage up your way, though?"

Jaxson shook his head. "World Heritage rainforest-meets-the-sea kind of deals tend to bring in the tree-huggy types."

"And?"

Jaxson lifted one shoulder, gestured toward his armpit, and then waved the hand toward his groin. "And I prefer a bit of landscaping, if you know what I mean."

His father grunted as he hauled up the next swimmer. "Smooth as a seal is what I'm hearing."

Jaxson rolled his eyes, indicating the argument had been hashed out before. "No, Dad, not that. Well, not necessarily." He shot a grin at Erik. "Though I'm not saying that's a definite no. Just that some of us have moved on from getting hard over the Amazons."

"Hells, Jax, you're not getting the old man started on about them again, are you? You know how he likes a trip down memory lane." The newcomer thumped Erik on the shoulder. "Cuz. How you been?"

"Ty, my man." With his cousins here, this council meeting could have some benefits, other than nutting out a plan to take down the fleet of illegal trawlers. And maybe getting his uncle to talk some sense into Trent about his plan to seek out the crew who'd maimed and tried to murder Jayde.

Her skin tawny alongside the more golden tan of the men, Elena stepped daintily from the pool, flicking her wrists to retract the rainbow-shimmering webbing between her fingers. "Hello, Erik."

Her voice was soft, almost demure. As always, he was struck by the permanent sadness in her eyes, a look of wishful longing that made no sense, given that she was always surrounded by men who only wanted to worship the sand she trod. Well, okay, that wasn't actually all he wanted to do with her, but a bit of foot kissing wouldn't be an unpleasant start.

Instead, he kissed her cheek, keeping his balance despite the nudge Tyson gave him from behind. "It's good to see you again, Elena." He ignored Jax's smothered guffaw, and before his dick could betray his interest—despite Elena's sedate one-piece swim costume revealing far too little—he swiveled back to his uncle. "You remember where the guest wing is? Help yourselves to rooms down there. I've got to head in for a shift now, but I'll be back by dinner. Trent's organized for some of the guys from The School to drop by after work tonight."

His uncle nodded, adjusting the waterproof pack all the Mer carried. "Where is Trent, then? Work?"

"Here." Trent's gravelly voice came from the tunnel leading into the chamber. He stepped just inside the rock arch and nodded at each Mer in turn. "Uncle. Guys. Elena, I'm really glad to see you here."

Jax snorted. "Yeah, no brainer."

Trent grinned, then stepped to one side, revealing the doorway. And the woman hidden behind his bulk, toying with the knot on the short sarong tied low around her hips. "Everyone, this is Jayde."

A frown swept his uncle's face, his rugged features stern. "She's not Mer?" Their numbers dwindling, the Mer were mostly known to one another, and their underwater locations were never revealed to humans.

Trent shook his head. "Not exactly." He drew himself up to his full height, one arm dropping to encircle the bikini-clad woman's waist, drawing her against his side. "But we're bonded."

Elena gasped, her eyes flashing from Trent to Jayde, her hand moving to cover her mouth. Tension crackled through the cave.

Jax stiffened. "Hot damn, no wonder you called the Council."

"WTF, dude?" Tyson drawled, shaking his head as he crossed his arms over his chest.

Erik winced. Damn, he'd have headed in to work early if he'd realized Trent planned to spring the news like this. "Way to go, Trent," he groaned. "You could've eased in with that one. Maybe a bit of a greeting, family catch-up first—"

Daniel strode forward, his fists clenched. "What the hell? This'd better be your idea of a joke."

Trent stood his ground as Erik snatched at his uncle's shoulder. "Wait up, Dan. Hear him out."

Daniel shook him off, his ice-blue eyes blazing. "What's to hear? Trent, you've traded immortality for *this*? I'm sorry." He gave a curt nod to Jayde. "No offense, but— Gods, Trent, what am I supposed to tell your mother?"

Trent shrugged. "I guess you could start by telling her Jayde and I are working on giving her grandkids. Or at least, we're practicing."

Tyson chuckled, his gaze ranging over Jayde's hourglass figure, but Daniel wasn't distracted. His rage echoed from the walls. "You think that'll soften the blow? That she'll be so thrilled, she'll happily accept that she'll now outlive her son?" He ran a hand over his face, his voice ragged. "Trent, I don't damn well understand. You're not an idiot. You know our laws. You know the price of taking a human as your mate."

Trent nodded. "I do. And it's a price I was more than willing to pay to be with Jayde. Thing is— Hey, guys." He broke off, eyeing his cousins and then loosely covering Jayde's ears with his hands. A grin crossed his face, and Erik realized his brother was enjoying the slow reveal. Ass. "You guys want to keep that filth to yourselves? Bad enough Jayde has to put up with hearing Erik's perverted imagination, she doesn't need stereo."

Erik snorted. "Pot, kettle, black, bro." In any case, from what he'd heard of Jayde, the perversions didn't belong only to the Mer.

Dan's hand dropped from his face, his eyes narrowed like he tried to peer through the sandy blur of a tide change. "Jayde can hear us? What do you mean?"

Trent moved behind Jayde, his arms encircling her waist and caging her against his chest. "Yeah, well, like I was saying, Dan. I was willing to pay the price, to lose immortality to bond with Jayde. But it turns out, she's part Mer."

Chapter Two

Krissy burrowed her toes deep into the sand as the sun sank, a hazy burnt-orange blur sandwiched between the blue ocean and layered slices of apricot, gray, and pink clouds. The sharp sugar-white crystals warming her feet, she pulled her knees up beneath her chin, wrapped her arms around her legs, and gazed across the water.

Moving here had been a good call. A fresh start. A great place to recreate herself, the way she wanted to be. The warmth of the tropics seemed to offer a freedom, stripping layers of inhibitions along with clothes. No one this far north knew her, except her sister—and she'd be the last person to make any kind of judgment.

Her gaze swept along the kilometers of curved beach, and then she twisted to check the rise of the green verge behind her. Though a handful of stragglers near the water's edge were clearly determined to eke the last snatch of sun from what was probably an annual holiday to the tropical paradise, she had the place mostly to herself.

This was her favorite time, the lull between the day's tourists and the lovers who'd take a stroll after dining alfresco at one of the tiny cafés beneath the swaying palm trees a few hundred meters back from the shoreline.

She reached beneath her T-shirt, unclipped her bra, and pulled it through the armholes, rolling her shoulders and groaning.

Sighed luxuriantly. As she leaned back on her hands, her breasts thrust forward, nipples instantly hard as they brushed the thin cotton of her shirt.

She checked the beach again, in both directions. A vast expanse of smooth sand, marred only by sandcastles and footprints, the odd bit of seawrack. Far to her left was a red flag planted in the shingle. There'd been a yellow one to her right, but as she watched, a lifeguard furled the banner and packed it on the back of a quad bike.

The bottom of the sun dipped into the sea, lighting a stairway across the calm surface.

But the air was still tropically warm.

She chewed on her bottom lip.

Did she dare?

After all, this was her new life. Her authentic life. Life lived the way *she* wanted it to be.

She grinned, slapped her hands together to dust off the sand, and then hiked her T-shirt over her head and dropped it behind her. Using the fabric as a pillow, she lay back, closing her eyes. If she kept them closed, maybe she could pretend she was totally down with public nudity. Almost-nudity, at least. In any case, it was the tropics; half the world went topless here, and no one looked twice. It's not like going topless was illegal. And if she wanted to be free, this was a tiny step in the right direction. Live for the moment, right?

To hell with what Brandon would've thought of her display—though she could imagine his outraged tone, the words he'd have used. "Slut" had been employed quite a bit as their relationship spiraled toward its ultimate doom.

With her eyes closed, her hearing was enhanced. In the palms behind her, rainbow lorikeets shrieked as they raided the mango trees. Far beyond her feet, down the gentle slope of the beach, the tide washed in and out in a soft, perpetual rhythm. A breeze whispered through the palm fronds and stirred across her sensitive nipples, tightening them exquisitely.

Warmed by the last of the sun and lulled by the pulsating motion of the sea, she relaxed, allowing herself to drift on memories and dreams, hovering between sleep and wakefulness.

She startled as sand squeaked near her ear. Disoriented, she smacked her palms onto the beach towel she lay on, shoving herself half-upright.

"Sorry." Dressed in the red board shorts and yellow jersey of the coastal lifeguards, a man stood over her, hand raised as if to calm her. "Didn't mean to scare you. I wanted to let you know the lifeguard station's closed for the day."

She squinted up at him, vaguely noting he was ridiculously tall, and blinked uncomprehendingly, her brain still fogged from sleep. "What?"

The lifeguard shoved aviators up into black hair, the sides faded up into a tousle of sea and salt. His gaze roamed the length of her body. "I figured maybe you were planning to go for a swim, so I wanted to warn you that the surf isn't patrolled after five. There's a pretty bad rip out there." He gestured with one hand, but his eyes remained on her. Or to be more precise, on her naked breasts.

She could easily cover them. Pretty much with one

hand, in fact. As Brandon had frequently pointed out, she wasn't exactly over-endowed in the boob department.

Yet something about this guy's brazenness appealed. He wasn't trying to sneak sly peeks from behind the protection of sunglasses; he was openly admiring her body. Her nipples hardened at his attention. She relaxed, leaning back, her elbows in the sand so her breasts jutted forward. "Precisely where is this hazard I should avoid?"

Still not turning away, the lifeguard hiked a thumb over his shoulder, a cocky grin tipping his lips. "That-a-way."

Blood and realization surged to her loins. The guy knew he'd been caught checking out her half-naked body, and he didn't give a damn.

And that was fucking hot.

She was so over men who were too emasculated to whistle at her and too intimidated to hold a door open, yet sought to disguise their own lost gender identity by defining how she should act.

A.k.a., Brandon.

She wanted a man who could match her. A man who knew what he actually wanted, not what he was supposed to want. A man confident enough to state his desires and able to accept a woman who knew her own.

Well, who maybe sort of knew her own.

Was coming to grips with her own? Yeah, that was more honest. She was a work-of-emancipation-in-progress.

The lifeguard's grin broadened. "Though it's not only the rips you want to look out for. I've known people to get into trouble pretty much anywhere it's wet."

She cocked an eyebrow. No doubt, this guy was definitely playing the game. "That's not particularly specific. I suspect there are quite a few…*wet* places to be found around here." Her heart beat fast at her daring, and she felt almost drunk with her unsuspected boldness. This was the new version of her. No more waiting for a guy to make a move, no more being too afraid to say what she really wanted.

Green eyes met hers, challenging and assessing. "True. That's why it's important to play safe. I'm sure you know the rules." He waved a hand between his red shorts and yellow long-sleeved T-shirt as he quoted the beach safety rules the east coasters grew up with. "Always stay between the red and the yellow."

She swallowed as his hand paused at his groin, drawing her eye. There was no mistaking that his loose board shorts were now uncomfortably—though by no means unpleasantly—snug. Angling her chin, she indicated the greenery behind them but didn't take her eyes from him. "The public service announcements up on the foreshore suggest it's wise never to fight a strong pull."

Sun-whitened streaks feathered out from the corners of his eyes. "I'm impressed you took the time to read the posters. Most tourists are in too much of a hurry to hit the beach."

She could explain she wasn't a tourist, but he didn't need to know. In fact, it was better he didn't know. "I find fulfillment's far superior if the anticipation is extended."

He shot her a grin, then his eyes ranged the thicket of mango, coconut, and date palms, as though checking whether they were visible from the town. He folded his arms across his chest, biceps stretching the jersey fabric. "Did you notice the FLAGS acronym on the posters? G is for 'Get someone to *come* with you.' "

Her heart flipped as though she'd downed a triple espresso. "So if I plan to get wet, I should do it in company?" she said, impressed she managed to keep her voice level. Holy crud, everything below her waist was liquid. She shouldn't have worn beige shorts as they had no hope of hiding what had to be a very visible damp spot, but to be fair, she'd not chosen her outfit with the expectation of being flirted into a hands-free orgasm.

She shook sand from her hand, then brushed her palm across her chest. Allowed her fingers to drift across her nipple, thrilling at the lifeguard's hissed intake of breath. "And the lifeguard station is closed? Do you have an issue with people going down after hours?" She tilted her head to indicate the surf *down* the slope of the beach. Wouldn't pay to be too obvious. Not yet.

His pupils flared. "No issue, but I occasionally stay back after work in case the desire strikes…"

She gestured at his shirt. "Are you allowed to wear that when you're not on duty? Or are you deliberately working the all-girls-are-into-a-man-in-uniform angle?" She screwed up her face in anticipation of a major turnoff.

The lifeguard plucked the fabric between his finger and thumb and raised one shoulder. "Wouldn't want you to think that was a deliberate move." He dropped his sunglasses onto the sand beside her, then snagged the neck of the jersey and hauled it over his head.

Well, okay, so there was no major turnoff moment here; in fact, the only *moment* was the one it took for the garment to clear his face, the one she totally needed to readjust her own face, so the drool of her perving was less evident. The skimming fabric revealed his tanned flesh inch-by-inch, a striptease sexier than anything she'd ever seen on the far-too-many hen's nights friends dragged her to. The V-cut either side of his flat stomach demanded her gaze dart down, but she'd already been captivated by a rock-hard six-pack, and— Oh. My. Fucking. God. Above a monochrome half-sleeve of a mermaid swimming up his bicep toward the full-masted galleon sailing across his left pec, the broadest shoulders she'd ever seen rippled and bulged as the lifeguard tossed aside his shirt.

Warm and rewardingly firm, the sand ground against her crotch as she squirmed. Running the tip of her tongue across her lips, she prayed her voice would come out a darn sight sexier than a croak. She nodded toward the lifeguard's arm. "Girlfriend?" Each strand of the willowy mermaid's hair seemed to move in an invisible ocean current, her body keening toward the ship in mute longing, hand outstretched. The image was so realistic it could've been a photograph, if not for the mythical subject matter.

He glanced at his shoulder, green eyes widening as though he'd forgotten the art, though that amount of intricate detail must've stung like a hundred box jellyfish. "Mother," he joked. He gestured at the sand. "Mind if I sit?"

"If that's the best plan you have." Screw it. The guy was hot as all heck, and she'd never see him again. *Live for the moment* supposedly her new mantra, it was about time she got a bit more proactive than simply chanting the words at her bug-eyed reflection in the mirror each morning.

Tiny sand pyramids formed between them as he sat. "I'm not real big on planning. I prefer to wing it."

"Sounds perfect." She rolled onto her side to face him. Just *happened* to allow her nipple to brush his bicep. That was the good thing about small boobs: control. "Life's too short for plans."

"Or long enough to make you realize how pointless they are."

"That's pretty deep."

He stretched beside her, lying on his hip and elbow, and reached to brush back the lock of hair that had fallen across her face. "You have amazing eyes."

A giggle bubbled in her throat. Sure, her eyes were a decent feature, but really, predictable much? She put a hand across his face, covering his eyes. "Uh-huh. And what color are they?"

His teeth flashed, toothpaste-ad-perfect. "Deep blush pink, almost tawny. Huge areola surrounding perfect tips, which are, hopefully, puckering even tighter as we speak. Begging for this—" His tongue slashed across her palm.

Fuuuuck. He was disarming. Not that she had any intention of putting up a fight.

The lifeguard's voice dropped lower. "And it seems they'd be the perfect handful."

"My eyes?"

"Wait, you think I'm cracking on to you with a totally lame compliment about your eyes? Wow." He smacked a palm against his chest, a waft of coconut oil rippling across her senses. "Wounded. Give a guy a little credit. Iyiiss is an ancient Atlantean word. Means nipples. By extension, can mean breasts."

She rubbed a hand across her forehead, trying to keep up with his teasing. "You speak Atlantean?" That wasn't a thing, was it? Why the hell couldn't she think straight?

He touched a finger to her lips, then traced the slight indent in her chin, grazing a trail down her throat before skimming, feather-light, along her clavicle. She only had to breathe and his wrist would brush her breast.

"Of course I do," he said. "Atlantean's the language of love."

She recoiled. "I'd have been more interested if it was the language of lust."

His fingers trailed lower, and his palm warmed the crescent of her breast. "Oh, I'm also fluent in Lustavanian."

"You're claiming to be good with your mouth?" She tried to find her breath as he leaned closer.

His lips found the sweet spot below her ear, the place that made her quiver as he murmured throatily, "I prefer to let the consumer be the judge."

"The consumer or the consumed?"

"Or is that consumee?" His lips moved against her neck, the tension palpable as she strove to pretend their innuendo wasn't entirely erotic.

"I always thought that was a French soup."

"A hot, wet foreplay to the main course. Three of my favorite things."

Okay, so she was the only one making any pretense, this guy was clearly all-in. She winced at the raucous caw of gulls overhead. Hopefully, they didn't signal the arrival of the evening fish-and-chip brigade on the beach, because she wasn't about to move away from a man who just might know how to finger all the buttons she wanted pushed.

"But should we debate language skills, or focus on...oral skills?" His teeth nipped her earlobe at the precise second his fingers found her aching nipple. Sparks arced through her, and she gasped, flexing to shove her breast more firmly into his hand.

His shadowed jaw igniting a trail of pinpricks, he tracked kisses across her breast, smoothing his hand down her ribcage as he exposed her nipple. He breathed against it, even warmer than the balmy caress of the tropical air. "Fuck," he muttered as the tight nub blossomed. "I have to have that." He paused a microsecond, as if to give her a chance to object, then his tongue flicked across her sensitive flesh.

"Oh, God," she moaned, sliding her fingers through the short hair at the nape of his neck, the fade bristly on her palms until she wound her fingers into the length on top, forcing him closer to her breast. "Oh, God, yes."

Brandon never spent time adoring her breasts, considering them an anatomical endowment designed solely for feeding his children.

Back before she'd told him she never planned to have kids.

And before he'd told her she wasn't woman enough to be able to feed babies, anyway. There'd been a lot of cruel words.

The lifeguard teased her with his tongue, his hand massaging her breast so all the sensation centered in the tight peak. "I want this in my mouth. I want to taste you," he growled, his lips vibrating against her puckered flesh. "Do you want me to? Tell me exactly what you want."

She'd never heard sexier words.

"This?" His tongue licked slowly across her nipple, and fireworks exploded in her belly. "Or this?" His palm pressed in the apex of her thighs. A slow, sexy, confident smirk tipped his lips. "Or this and this?" His mouth found her nipple again, his teeth grazing the flesh, the slight pain heightening the exquisite pleasure of his suckling. At the same moment, his hand slipped beneath the waistband of her shorts, his finger stroking across her thin underwear.

She gasped, snatching at the sand as her hips bucked up to his touch. Dammit, why the heck had she worn underwear?

He gripped her panties, drawing the fabric into a thin strip pulled tight against her clit and anus. "Is this what you want? Are you going to come for me before I even touch you?"

No. But any second now she'd come for herself.

He bunched the material tighter, sliding one finger along the smooth, swollen lips he exposed. Grinned wolfishly. "Damn. Brazilian? I want to see this."

And she wanted him to.

She moved her hands to her hips, pushing against her shorts, but he bent to her other breast.

"I'm not done with these yet," he said. Taking her nipple between his teeth, he drew back. Spikes of pain and desire and urgency shot through her. She arched, thrusting her center against his hand, desperate for him to plunge his fingers inside her, to frig her, to make her *feel*. God, just one finger would do, she was so damn close.

Coconut and salt wafted as he shifted, his stubble sandpapering her cheek. "You're going to come if I do this, aren't you?" His finger brushed her clit, only the taut fabric separating their flesh.

"Yesss," she hissed, closing her eyes and giving herself over to the sensation as the pressure mounted. "Oh, yes!"

Her eyes sprang open as his lips touched hers. Knees clamped together quicker than a rabbit trap, she turned her head aside.

He drew back, quirking an eyebrow. "No kissing?"

"No." That was where the possessiveness always started.

"Fair enough. But it's still all right if I do this?" He watched her as his tongue circled her darkened nipple.

She wound her fingers into his hair but groaned as sand speckled them both. "Ugh. You know what's wrong with sex on the beach?"

"Worst name for a candle fragrance, period?"

"Yeah, well, there is that. But the sand. Sand is not sexy. Grit gets into…well, everything. Total mood killer." Dammit, why was she talking now? Why had she let the sudden rush of nerves, a pathetic concern about being once again owned, spoil the moment?

"Wow. Way to destroy the fantasy of a holiday romance for thousands of people. Hope you're not a copywriter."

She snorted. "Sorry, am I cutting your out-of-hours perks? Someone needs to tell it like it is. Fantasies are the biggest con of all time. They belong with rainbow-pooping unicorns, fairies, and…and"—she jabbed a finger at his mermaid tattoo—"those. We're indoctrinated at birth into believing we have to chase a fairytale to be happy, conditioned to think we need to find Mr. Right, marry, have our two-point-three kids, and then life will be happily-ever-after. And you know what? We're so busy waiting for the mythical fantasy to begin, we forget to live in the *now*." Oh, what the hell? *Seriously, shut up, Krissy*. This guy didn't need a dose of her verbal diarrhea, even if it was the truth.

The lifeguard withdrew his hand from her shorts and shifted away from her, lying on his side. "Ah. That's a hint you want me to back off."

She clambered to her feet, the move nowhere close to elegant. Darn it, why had she given up yoga? "Not at all. I don't do hints." Not this new version of her, anyway. "It was an invitation to come and get wet with me." She shucked her shorts and kicked them toward her T-shirt.

The lifeguard rose lithely. He probably did yoga. And tai chi. And weights. "Phrased like that, there's no way I'm saying no."

The ocean had extinguished the sun, twilight falling soft and thick, a velvet curtain sprinkled with diamantes. He reached for her hand. "This way. The shallows hide a few rocks on that side."

She hadn't noticed the size of his hands before. Huge. But she'd been right about his height, the thigh-deep water skimming his knees.

"Too cold?" he said.

The temperature wasn't why she shivered. She shot him a glance, hoping to ace sultry rather than deer-in-the-headlights terrified, took a breath, and then plunged beneath the dark surface. She breast-stroked a few feet and then stood, waist-deep in the water.

Completely alone. The ocean's surface millpond calm no matter which direction she looked. Arms crossed over her breasts, she gazed around, the water dark and ominous, the silence eerie.

Where had he gone?

A lifeguard, he wouldn't have gotten caught in a rip.

Would he?

A flash of blue light about a hundred meters farther out to sea caught her eye. "How the heck did you get all the way out there?" she called, hoping it was him.

"Practice." His voice rolled across the waves. "Come on out; it's warmer where it's deeper."

"It isn't safe."

"You'll be safe with me. I promise."

She shook her head, though he wouldn't be able to see. "Nuh-uh. There are bitey things out there."

"Only me." He chuckled, somehow propelling himself quickly through the water without splashing. Nothing like her drowning-frog mix of dog-paddle and slightly panicked breaststroke.

The water eddied around her as he drew near. "The beach is shark-netted."

"Oh, look," she gasped, pointing at his torso. Beneath the water, he glittered with phosphorescence like he'd been spattered with a blue glowstick at a nightclub. "Is that the coral spawn or something?"

He shrugged as he stood, droplets journeying from his shoulders, down the cliffed overhang of his pecs. "Some kind of marine-life weird-out, I guess."

"But I'm not glow—"

His hands grasped her hips, the water buoying her against his firm body. His entirely unmistakable and far-from-inconsequential erection pressed into her stomach. A couple more nudges from that thing and she'd be glowing, all right.

Fingers working up the nape of her neck and into her hair, he mouthed at the pulse in her throat, his lips pressing in a firm, erotic rhythm with the racing beat of her heart. "Is this okay?"

She closed her eyes, tilting her head back. "Very okay. Anything except kissing."

"Anything?" His other hand slid over the angle of her hip and down, cupping her buttock.

Nerves and excitement flitted through her stomach. She was in control of what would happen. She could ask—no, *demand*—what she wanted. And if he thought her kinky or perverted or any of the many slurs Brandon had thrown her way, it didn't matter. She'd never see this guy again.

Sliding her hand between them, she brushed her palm over his bulging shorts. According to her limited experience—based almost entirely on online porn—the guy was hung. And his current state was due to her presence. A surge of confidence curved her lips. "How well can you float?"

"You'd be surprised." His fingers whispered down the crack of her ass.

She quivered, resisting the urge to jut her butt out Insta-star-style, and closed her left hand over his shaft, wedged vertical between them. "Show me."

"Ah," he grunted. "Is that an 'I'll show you mine if you show me yours' kind of proposition?"

She chuckled, toying with the piercing that anchored the galleon sailing across his chest. "I mean, show me how well you can float. Though if you're offering…"

"Oh, I'm offering all right." His cock twitched in her hand. She clenched her fist tighter, slowly pumping him.

His hand closed over hers, stopping her movement, and he blew out a short breath. "Float, huh?"

"Yes." She let go of his nipple ring, flattening her palm over his hammering heart. Increasing the pressure, she pushed him back until he lay in the water, though it almost seemed he lay *on* it. He placed his hands beneath his head and crossed his ankles, floating as if he were on an inflatable lounge.

"Nice sail." She nodded at his tented pants. "You'll definitely catch the breeze."

He bent his knees, dropping his feet as though he'd stand, but she shook her head. "Not yet." She pushed him farther out into the ocean so he floated level with the perky breasts he reached a dripping hand to fondle, her nipples achingly hard as his thumb brushed across them.

Her hand swept from his chest, across the hard ridges of his abs, and down his flat stomach. Heat radiated through her palm, up her arm, and oozed into her core, centering in her groin with the weight of a cannonball.

Maybe realizing how vulnerable he was, despite his size, the lifeguard tensed as her exploring hand reached the low-slung waist of his shorts. She hooked her fingers in the fabric and dragged the material down.

His cock sprang free.

And she was right.

It was massive.

And well, gorgeous, corded with thick ridges, as

though specifically designed to bring pleasure. To her. She licked her lips and glanced at his face, reading his emotions. Lust. Excitement. Urgency surged in her. She wanted him. In so many ways.

Fingers closing around his shaft, she bent and swirled her tongue over his throbbing helmet. He tasted good. Salty and warm, and she couldn't stifle her moan of pleasure. Yeah, not even with that mouthful. She sucked him in a little, curling her tongue around the bulging head of his cock, her teeth grazing the tight skin before allowing him to pop free.

"God," he grunted, his hips surging toward her retreating mouth. Water splashed across his tense abdomen.

"Hold still, or you'll go under," she ordered.

"I'm not the one going down." The joke strained through gritted teeth, the muscles in his neck tense as he lifted his head to watch her.

She angled so she could see his face as she worked her tongue over his sensitive frenulum, caressing the dip in the top of his cock. Sucked him in.

He pulsed within her mouth. Groaned. His hand moved to the back of her head, but he snatched it back, fisting it at his side, a sheet of phosphorescence sluicing across his belly. "Sorry."

Keeping her lips tight, she drew back, releasing his prick an inch at time. "Don't be." She was over being sorry for what she wanted. He should feel the same. "Grab my head. I want you to fuck my mouth."

It was the dirtiest thing she'd ever said, almost the dirtiest she'd ever thought, and the freedom of hearing her own words, of voicing her desire, turned her on. Her labia swelled against the sensual caress of the cool current, her fist sliding up and down his smooth penis.

"Are you serious? Oh, fuck, yes!" His fingers wound into her hair as she bent to take his cock, gagging as it hit the back of her throat.

Her eyes watered, only partly from the salt water splashing her face as the lifeguard's thrusts dipped his hips beneath the water. One hand squeezing his balls, she set a punishing rhythm with the other, pumping him into her mouth. Hollowing her cheeks to increase the suction each time she pulled his cock out, she gasped for breath, her thumb swirling through his pre-cum.

He was panting almost as hard as she was, chest heaving, eyes unblinking as he watched her head bobbing up and down. His balls tightened in her hand, and she pulled back. Grinned at the flash of disappointment on his face. Took a long, slow lick right up the shaft of his dick, then sucked on the throbbing head, letting it pop from her lips like a lollipop. She fastened her gaze on his. "I want you to come in my mouth."

"Jesus!"

She didn't give him time to think, but double fisted him, clamping her lips over his engorged cock as she fucked it into her mouth.

"Gods, baby, I'm going to—"

She didn't know whether he was promising or warning, but his thick cream spurted deep in her throat as her own orgasm hit, buckling her knees so she sagged against him. She milked his cock a couple of times, but then backed off, the silvery strands spurting onto her face and chest as she caught her breath.

As he groaned, she scooped the cum from her chin. Smeared it across her lips. Chased it with her tongue.

Total power play.

Because no one would ever again tell her what she was allowed to do.

Chapter Three

He couldn't get his damn shorts back up quick enough. Somehow, they'd ended up tangled and twisted around his legs, and the girl was splashing through the shallows as he floundered and swallowed water. Some Mer he was.

Reciting a couple of centuries' worth of well-honed curses in his head, he gave up with the pants and called after her. "Hey, do you want to give me your number?"

She halted with her back to him for a moment, the world silent except for the wash of the ocean. A gleam of silver in the moonlight, she turned toward him. "I don't think either of us is packing a pen."

"I'll memorize it."

She grinned and shook her head. "That's not how this works." Then she spun back to the beach and strode from the water.

"Wait. What's your name?" Damn it, what was he doing? He and Trent had a rule—well, they'd *had* a rule, until Jayde came along—about never asking a girl's name. Didn't pay to get her hopes up, and in any case, one night of shagging by two Mer was enough for any chick. Names became numerous and irrelevant.

Yet now he sounded like a teenager, begging for crumbs to flesh out a fantasy.

And the woman ignored him, her butt sashaying alluringly as she strode up the beach, lifting a hand in greeting to a pair of late-evening joggers. As though she wasn't wearing just a pair of black panties and her face hadn't been smeared with his cum seconds before.

Gods. That was his kind of woman.

She'd dressed and left the beach by the time he'd pulled himself together, shoving his dick back into his shorts. Still half-hard because, the second he touched it, he was reminded of her soft hands, her sucking, tormenting, promising mouth, and he barred up again.

He picked up his shirt, phone, and shoes from where he'd dropped them in the sand, and headed back to the lifeguard station. He needed a drink.

Inside the upper-level office overlooking the ocean, he crossed to the communal fridge. Groaned. The stock of beer and soft drinks reminded him that what he *actually* needed was to pick up groceries and get back to The Cavern. Somehow, he'd lost over an hour of his evening—an hour he'd willingly lose a million times over—and now he wouldn't have time to swing past the apartment and take care of the horde before the Mer meeting.

Still, Jax probably wouldn't take too much persuasion to head back in with him later in the evening, when the cafés morphed into bars oozing live music and wreathed in particularly fragrant smoke, and the coastal strip became a fairyland—not that the Fae were keen on the comparison—of twinkling lights strung between the trees where the millennials came out to play.

The live-it-up-before-the-apocalypse, avocado-on-toast crew generally provided good fishing.

Hopefully, he could reel in a whole lot more of what he'd just had.

****

Droplets rolled from his skin as though it were oiled, and his hair dried quickly as he stepped from The Cavern's entry pool. He strode down the tunnel, tugging off his waterproof backpack. Took out the cakes he'd purchased and slung them into Davy Jones' Locker. For once in a decade, the icebox was stocked. Trent and Jayde had obviously found time to head ashore.

Pausing his movements—and even his breathing—to focus his thoughts, he searched for the other Mer. Found them in the smaller meeting room, where they congregated unless it was the formal Senior Council meeting. The presence of about a dozen voices proved the guys from The School were already there.

He ducked into his room and dragged on light chinos and a fresh long-sleeved T-shirt. One of the benefits of the subterranean cave system was that the temperature varied little. To notice a substantial difference, he'd have to track hundreds of kilometers through the caves, until he was beneath the Antarctic icecaps. Not much chance of that.

Give him the sun-drenched tropics and bikini-clad chicks anytime.

Or shorts-clad chicks.

He adjusted his own pants as his mind strayed back to the beach. Quickly he blocked his thoughts.

Apparently, not quickly enough. Tyson chuckled as Erik entered the meeting room, and Jax affected a hurt look. "Dude, fishing without me? After I traveled all this way, too."

"I'll make it up to you." He grinned as he took his seat at the oval table. "Soon as we get done here, in fact. Guys." He raised his chin, acknowledging the rest of the Mer. "And ladies." Well, that plural was one out of the box. Though their mother would sometimes drop by, any other female in this southern extension of The Cavern was a rare occurrence. Two women at the same time? Unheard of. "What are we up to?"

Jax snorted. "Well, we know what you've been up to, and we're just about to catch up with what your bro's been up to. Hopefully with all the spicy detail, because, though I'm probing her, it seems Jayde's already pretty good at blocking her thoughts."

Erik glanced at Jayde, seated close to Trent on the opposite side of the table, his arm draped protectively around her shoulders. The color rose in her cheeks, but she met his eye. A week ago, she'd not been so good at masking her thoughts from the Mer telepathy.

He shot her a message. *Don't worry, they're gonna shit stir until they get the measure of you. They don't mean any harm.*

She nodded and let down her shield for a moment to reply. *I know, just still weird being able to feel people listening to my thoughts.*

Soon you'll be able to pick and choose who you let in.

The chatter among the Mer died as Daniel spoke. "Sorry, Jayde. We'll try to keep the habit under control. It can be exceedingly invasive." He cast a stern eye around the table, lingering on his sons. "But it's rarer than a frilled shark to hear a fresh voice, and we're intrigued to hear your story."

As all eyes focused on her, Jayde blushed deeper. "I'm not sure where to start—"

Hand on her shoulder, Trent stood. "For anyone

who missed it, Jayde's part Mer, and she's a marine biologist." From his tone, his brother might've announced his bond-partner had won the Nobel Peace Prize, though it was hard to tell which part of her bio he was more proud of. It was clear he figured he'd sure as hell won himself a prize.

Which was fine, if you were into being tied down. Didn't float Erik's boat at all.

The Mer around the table nodded, though their interest would be more in the part-Mer revelation. With Mer drawn to the ocean and ecology, plenty of them worked in Jayde's professional field. But part Mer? In any profession? Unheard of. What Mer would trade immortality to spend a shortened eternity with a human?

Except Trent, of course.

"So how did you meet?" Elena's soft voice would probably have been missed among the rumbles of interest, if it hadn't been unusual to hear a female at any except the most Senior Council meetings.

Trent's lips narrowed in sudden anger, his grip tightening on Jayde's shoulder. "Jayde was scuba diving on the reef. She found a dolphin calf hooked on a trawler longline."

"Longline on the reef?" Daniel straightened. "There's no licensing for that."

"Exactly," Jayde agreed. "With the reef already under stress from climate change, there shouldn't be *any* kind of fishing allowed. The Marine Protection Agency is a damned joke, and the government's clearly selling out, approving fossil fuel projects and deep-water fracking. We can't afford to let the longliners push the boundary on this." Her voice rose, her spine stiffening. "We need to fight to preserve the few restrictions the government has in place. Once the reef is compromised, it'll take millennia to restore."

"Good point," Daniel said, and Erik caught the flare of pride in Trent's mind. Daniel picked up the pen sitting diagonally across the notepad in front of him. "Any chance you were able to get a name on this trawler? We'll run the usual interference."

"Wait. It's more than that." Trent's chest rose raggedly, and Elena winced at the palpable anger radiating from him. His fingers left pale lines as he rubbed a hand across his tanned face.

Erik had seen Jayde when Trent rescued her. He knew what distressed his brother.

Eyes closed, Trent allowed a mental image to form and commed it to the group.

"Gods!" Carl, a senior lifeguard from The School, thrust back from the table, as though he could distance himself from the mind-picture of Jayde's beaten, bloodied body.

Jayde shot a confused look at her bond-partner. Clearly, Trent hadn't allowed her to see his memory.

Erik picked up his twin's jumbled, agonized thoughts and stood. "Jayde rescued the calf but was hooked herself. The trawler hauled her up." He needed to keep this factual, get the details out there, instead of having Trent dwell on what had happened to the woman he was destined to spend his life with. "Seems the crew felt her injury might implicate them, probably evidence their illegal activity." He searched for moisture in his dry mouth. "So they beat her and threw her overboard. Even without the sharks, her injuries would've been fatal if Trent hadn't found her."

Elena reached past Carl, her hand closing on Jayde's forearm. "Gods. I'm so sorry, Jayde. That must have been terrifying. For your own people to treat you like that—"

Jayde shook her head, memory clouding her eyes. She crossed her arms over her chest, hugging her elbows. "Not *my* people. Not anymore. Humans. Except—" She glanced up at Trent, as though seeking permission. He nodded. "Except one. I didn't see him, but the guy who attacked Trent and then locked him up to die when he was shot…he was Mer."

Instant uproar filled the room.

"What the hell? A Mer?" Tyson bellowed.

Daniel stood as well, the room crowded with giants. "You were attacked, Trent? You repaired, obviously."

Trent pressed close behind Jayde, as though the physical contact reassured him of her presence. Erik felt a stab of guilt at having teased his brother earlier. Though, really, the dick deserved it, if only to make up for all the occasions Trent had shit-stirred him.

"Repaired, but only thanks to Jayde," Trent said.

Daniel frowned. Mer were almost immortal. "Are you sure the attacker was Mer?"

"Oh, that bastard was Mer all right. He knew depriving me of water was the best way to kill me."

"So Jayde found you, gave you water?" Jax nodded. "Sweet."

Fine lines creased the edges of Trent's green eyes, and Erik snorted with laughter.

Don't you dare, Jayde telepathed to her mate, a flush rushing up her cheeks.

A slow smile crossed Trent's face. "Jayde found a

38

way to…hydrate me. And you're right, it was sweet."

"Maybe TMI, bro," Erik cautioned as curiosity from the other Mer eddied through his head.

What Jayde had done would become legend among them soon enough, but though his brother would lay down his life to protect his bondmate, he was crazy-proud of her initiative. His urge to boast was about to overrule his common sense.

Erik picked up the thin file of printed sheets that lay in front of him. "Thing is, we got the name of the trawler, and I ran it through the system. It's part of a fleet. And we're thinking, if one ship in the fleet is rogue, what are the chances the others are abiding by the law? Jayde and Trent boarded *Poseidon's Nemesis*—" He paused to allow the explosion of interest.

His uncle's eyes turned to flint. "*Poseidon's Nemesis*? This rogue Mer owns the vessel, then?"

Erik lifted one shoulder. "The name of the boat sure seems like a deliberate jab at Gramps, but the records aren't easily accessible. At least, not online. Privacy laws, I guess." He passed printed sheets around the table. "I tracked down the name of the skipper, but the full ownership details weren't available. I did manage to source the names of the sister vessels registered to the same corporate entity, though." As the Mer scanned the information he'd passed out, he took a deep breath, exchanging a relieved look with Trent.

There was a chance they'd imagined a conspiracy theory, following Jayde's assault aboard *Poseidon's Nemesis*, but the muttered incredulity of the Mer made it clear they interpreted the list the same way he and Trent had.

"*The Cronus. The Zeus. The Athena.*" He punctuated each name on his page with a stab of his finger.

Trent shoved his sun-bleached surfie dreads back, shifting his feet to stand wide. "Even if that Mer bastard isn't the owner, it looks like we've been sold out. Too much of a fluke that all these vessels are named after Poseidon's enemies, don't you think?"

"How do you mean, 'sold out'?" Isaak drawled. He'd transferred to The School from the USA south coast the previous year, and the guys amused themselves by employing deliberate Australianisms to confuse him.

Now, however, no one made a joke.

Daniel blew out his cheeks, a line furrowing his forehead. "The names are a red flag that the operators are on to us. A deliberate taunt."

Erik poured water from a pitcher on the table but didn't drink. "That's what we figured. It's a setup. We're just not sure whether they're warning us to stay clear, or daring us to take them on."

Elena gasped. "You think the Mer from the trawler broke the pact and informed on us?"

"It looks that way," Daniel said.

"But why would he do that?" Her face flushed and then went oddly pale.

Daniel pinched the bridge of his nose. "Until we find out *who* he is, we have to assume his motivation is money. His betrayal will have been well compensated, because it's bought the fleet the ability to fish wherever and however they want. We daren't take action against them, or we'll be exposed. Without saying a word, they can blackmail our compliance, force us to turn a blind eye to them raping the ocean."

Erik nodded. Five-hundred-plus years of experience sure made a guy quick on the uptake. "We can't risk the exposure. Look what happened to the *Rainbow Warrior*, hunted down and sunk by the French Intelligence because they failed to stay beneath the radar. Two men lost."

Trent's fist slammed the table. "Thing is, if the rogue Mer sold us out to this fleet owner, what's to stop him going wide with the information?" He glanced around, making contact with each Mer, probing their minds, and evoking their race memories.

His words dropped like ballast stones into Arctic waters. "I'm sure we all recall what it was like to be hunted."

Chapter Four

Krissy edged the wooden platters, each holding six small, half-filled glasses of beer, in front of the three customers seated on stools at the high outdoor table. Who even ordered tasters a half-hour before closing? The hipsters would end up slamming the shots down and then, unable to decide which they liked, yell for a schooner of each right on last call. Which meant they'd be shit-faced, and she couldn't lock up her side of The Little Blue until well after knock-off. Again. A breeze stirred around her thighs, flipping at the hem of her sarong-style skirt.

"Keep the change." One of the guys slid a fifty across the slab bench toward her.

Darn, but she did love Americans, though. Aussies didn't tip. Transferring her day job from the city to the smaller office farther north had been the best idea ever, if moving up the seaboard meant her second job came with the chance of cash on the side for the cost of a cute smile. She'd kind of accidentally adopted a stray kitten she'd found shivering in a tropical rainstorm beneath the café dumpster, and her sister was less than thrilled at the prospect of an extra mouth to feed. With tips like this, she'd be able to afford to have the flea-bitten bundle vet-checked in a week or so. Even if that meant ramen for dinner for the next month.

She leaned forward to collect the note. Snapped

upright. Cute smile? Yeah, right. Apparently, the exchange rate was handful-of-ass, and the short uniform provided easy access for this sleaze. The hipster's manscaped beard nudged his chest as he winked.

Ice clipped her tone. "Don't pay me. I'll send the manager out with your check." There was a vast difference between appreciating a guy who was confident enough to flirt and allowing one who thought his ten-buck tip equated to paying for additional services. The threat of management presence generally worked, patrons happier to give up a grope than relinquish their craft beer.

Not this one.

He tightened his hand. "Don't bother with that, hon. I'm not done yet. Might need to top up that bill. Especially if you add a bit of sugar."

As he tugged her closer, his beard prickling her padded-bra-enhanced cleavage, she snatched one of the glasses and upended it on his black skinny jeans.

So the movies lied. In real life, with a table full of drunken hipsters and a taster-sized drink, the cool-off was ineffective, to say the least.

"Hon, if you want to make me all juicy, I'm sure we can arrange something." The guy's breath blasted her face, and she winced. He might've only just lobbed up at her bar, but he'd clearly hit several earlier in the evening.

As his hand slid from her butt to between her legs, panic fluttered in her chest. With five years' experience, she could generally handle the guys who'd had a bit too much fun. They either needed their egos padding or slapping into place. But rarely did they get this physical.

She glanced toward the palm-thatched café, through cantilevered doors folded open to maximize the ocean breeze. On the far side of the long bar, both Adele and Shayn worked the busier section overlooking the ocean, leaving her with the secluded courtyard beneath the trees. Only three of her tables were currently occupied.

The drunk's other arm trapped her waist, his fingers burrowing against her panties.

Dropping the glass, she hauled back, putting her full weight behind a stinging slap. "Let me go, you bloody Neanderthal!"

An angry red stain etching his cheek, he snatched her wrist. "Like to play rough, do—?"

Hands seized Krissy's waist from behind, swinging her away from the table, her view blocked by a man's back as he positioned himself between her and her customers. Controlled fury iced the newcomer's tone. "If a girl says no, you listen. Touch her again without permission, and that'll be sexual assault."

She knew that voice. Even from behind, she recognized the spread of his shoulders, muscles rippling beneath a thin T-shirt as he braced. She'd deliberately stayed away from the beach for the last two days.

But that didn't mean she hadn't thought about him.

Pretty much all the darn time.

Hence the new nickname for her vibrator: the lifeguard.

The other tables cleared in a rush and scuffle of overturned chairs. The hipster sneered but scooted off his stool. "By the time you level a charge, I'll be out of the country."

The lifeguard folded brawny arms across his chest,

the short sleeves stretched over his biceps. "The airlines won't fly you with life-threatening injuries. Sit down!" he barked as the hipster's buddies tried to circle in behind him.

They sat.

He angled to include her, his chin indicating the fifty lying on the table. "Is that all they owe?"

She licked her lips to find her voice. "That's ten extra."

"They only gave you a ten-dollar tip? Between the three of them?"

"Oh!" she gasped as the hipster let fly with an illegal coward punch, aiming for the back of the lifeguard's head.

The fist connected, but the lifeguard barely reacted. Just a slow blink of his sea-green eyes and the ghost of a smile as he turned to his assailant. "You shouldn't have done that. But I'm stoked you did. *Now* I get to play."

Quicker than Krissy could follow the movements, certainly faster than such an enormous man should be able to move, the lifeguard grabbed the hipster's balled fist, spun the guy around, and twisted his arm up behind his back. "You have a free hand. Get your wallet out. Put it on the table. You two as well." He jerked a hard jaw at the other two men. "Pull your cash out."

As they complied, he yanked the hipster's arm higher. "Right, you get to toss a hundred into the pot. You two can contribute fifty a piece."

"No!" She dashed in front of the lifeguard. "They didn't do anything. It was only this dickhead."

The lifeguard lifted one shoulder, his expression far from conciliatory. "They may not have done anything, but I didn't see them preventing anything, either."

If she took the money, the hipster won; he'd paid for a grope. The world's most expensive grope, sure, but still, he'd bought what he wanted. No way was she allowing that to happen. "I don't want their money. Just the forty dollars they owe the café for their bar tab."

"If you don't let them pay, then I'll still need to punish them."

She wasn't sure if he was serious. Despite his easy humor and flirting the other day, the angry version of the lifeguard was kind of terrifying.

And totally damn hot.

Her teeth worried at her lip. The lifeguard could wind up in prison for assault if she didn't allow him to make his point in a nonviolent way. "There's a marine protection fund on the counter." She pointed toward the café. "They can make a donation."

"Perfect," the lifeguard drawled. "You take their money. I want to have a few words with them." His eyes glittered ominously.

She scooped up the two hundred dollars and raced into the café. Rang forty into the till, then took the rest over to the plastic collection box. Her hand hovered over the donation slot. The money would cover Seagull's vet check and maybe even desexing.

But it wasn't hers.

She stuffed the cash into the box and whirled away.

The three customers stood in a line, errant schoolboys in front of the headmaster. Gazes nailed to the ground, wallets nowhere in sight, they didn't look up as she approached.

The lifeguard did, though, his gaze caressing her

from head to foot. And that glance made her feel all kinds of things, and not one of them was bad.

Not anymore, not in her new life.

He smiled. "These guys now seem to be aware of where they went wrong. They'd like to apologize. Is there a particular form you prefer?"

Way to put her on the spot. "Abject groveling is always good, I guess." Like she'd know.

"Done." He swiveled back to the men. "You heard the lady. On your knees."

Two of them dropped instantly, the third assisted by a foot to the back of his knees. They muttered their apologies.

A sardonic grin twisted the lifeguard's lips. "Okay, then, off you go. Enjoy the rest of your vacation." A frown played between his dark brows as he watched the men scurry away, then turned to look down at her. "I'll wait until you finish up, then see you home."

The thought of him coming back to her place, well, more like to her bed, thrilled through her, warming places that had already spent far too much of the last couple of days tingling.

She folded her arms across her chest. It was one thing to let her desire rule, but entirely another to allow him to think he had some kind of responsibility for her. "I didn't need rescuing, you know."

"It's kind of my job, *you know*."

"Thought that only applied to the water?"

"Thought I made it clear I'd operate anywhere it's wet?"

Laughter rippled through her. If she kept him at arms' length—though most definitely not in a literal sense—this guy could be fun. Had already been fun.

He stepped closer. "So tell me about this abject groveling. You like a man on his knees?"

She assessed him for a long moment, trying to act chill while she prayed for her brain to catch up and put something in her mouth that wouldn't come out sounding like a lustful moan. "I, er, I—" *Yeah, thanks brain, total lustful moan.* "I'm done here. Let me cash up, and then I'll show you how much I like a man on his knees. Or rather, I'll let you show me."

"Hell, yeah." The appreciation in his tone was unmistakable, and her self-confidence soared. Screw Brandon—or preferably, don't screw Brandon—he was wrong. There was nothing unnatural about her desires and no reason for her to deny them.

She packed up fast, filled in her time sheet, and then dragged her boss out to where the lifeguard sat waiting for her at the table beneath the palms. "Adele, this is—"

"Erik," Adele purred.

"Hey, 'Dele." Erik lifted a hand.

"You know each other?"

"Sure, hon," Adele said, smoothing her tie-dyed shirt over her impressive bosom. "The guys from The School hang out here all the time."

"The School?" At least she had the guy's name now, without sharing hers. That was *not* the way she was playing this game. No name, no number, no tie.

"The lifesaving club," Erik said.

"Ah. School. As in fish, right? I get it." She pulled out her phone. "Mind if I take your picture?"

Erik quirked an eyebrow. "Notches on your bedpost?"

"Self-protection. I'm sending it to Adele, so if

you're an ax murderer, you're in deep shit."

He looked impressed. "Fair enough."

Adele's phone pinged. "Got it." She tipped her head to one side, checking the picture out. "Nice. I'm sure you're in safe hands, though. Don't do anything I wouldn't do, hon."

As Adele was a gently rounded, soft-voiced spinster in her forties, Krissy totally planned to do things her boss wouldn't.

Excitement fluttered in her chest. And yeah, a whole hell of a lot lower. She'd spent too long subduing her desires, allowing Brandon to label her urges depraved as he molded her into the perfect Stepford wife. In Erik's "safe hands" she'd discover what lust had to offer.

As Adele headed back into the café, Krissy looked up at Erik. "We can't go back to mine, I share. Do you have somewhere?"

He glanced at his watch. "I do. But I'm expecting a mate to drop by."

The palm tree behind him was suddenly fascinating as she willed the color that heated her chest to stay below the neck of her blouse. Her voice came out a little high. "That could work out well." If her heart pounded any harder, the frittata she'd inhaled for dinner would reappear.

"Excellent." Erik's sexy drawl was smooth and rich, cream on coffee.

And she did love cream. She thumbed her phone and scrolled to her sister's name. *Heading out. Could you please, please, pretty please, feed Seagull?*

The reply came instantly. *Staying back to make sure everything's ready for the auditor, remember? Will be a couple of hours, yet. Please do not let that monster destroy my house.*

She sucked an annoyed breath between her teeth.

Erik touched her elbow. "Something I can help with?"

She jumped at the contact. Not that he startled her, but because her flare of desire was instant. Pavlov's dog kind of instant. Though it wasn't her mouth that was salivating, Erik was welcome to ring her bell anytime. Letting him know where she lived didn't fit in with her plan of remaining elusive, but it was clear her loins had zero interest in maintaining any space between them, emotional or otherwise. "I have to duck home for a minute. It's only a block away." She gestured toward a back street, the purple night-shaded trees rustling with hunting fruit bats.

"Like I said, I'll walk you. If that's okay. I'd rather you didn't wander around alone until your new friends are at the airport. Check-in opens at six tomorrow morning, and I have it on good authority they'll be there nice and early."

"Okay. My place, then yours," she said.

"I like your energy."

She grinned. "I meant, my place because I have to do something there."

"Uh huh," he said. "And then my place, because I *really* have to do something there."

His hand brushed hers as they strolled, sticking to the center of the road to avoid the mangos littering the footpath, their honeyed fragrance thick in the air. Each touch brought a jolt of desire and anticipation. After years of Brandon's PDA bans, she'd forgotten the tilting, swirling thrill of sexual attraction, the breathtaking expectancy of an imminent hookup.

She led Erik to the rear yard of the old Queenslander she and her sister rented, and up the rickety stairs. Like many of the ancient weatherboards, the house was built on stilts to avoid the seasonal floodwaters.

Seagull made a dash for her as she unlocked the door, yowling and weaving around her ankles. She picked up the tabby-and-white splotched kitten, snuggling him to her chest as she fought to open a sachet of food.

"Here, give him to me." Erik took the kitten, tiny in one of his hands. "Cute little feller. Looks a bit young for solids, though."

"He doesn't think so." She placed the food bowl on the floor. "And he doesn't have a choice. A cat got run over outside work last week. I think she was his mum, though I couldn't find any other kittens. I'll take him to the vet as soon as I can."

Erik put the animal down. The kitten growled to protect his food, yet purred at the same time, desperate for affection.

She knelt to stroke his fur. "Calm down, Seagull. No one's taking it off you."

"Seagull? For the markings?"

"That, and the god-awful noise he makes when he's after food." She gave the kitten one last stroke and stood. "Sorry, that's enough of the crazy cat lady." *Nice work.* She'd laid both the cat's sob story and her anti-fantasy rant on him in the space of two brief meetings. At least there'd never be a risk of Erik getting attached.

"Don't apologize. You won't believe what I'm going to show you." Erik offered his hand as she stood, and then tugged her close, his hard body exuding more heat than the tropical sun.

If he'd forgotten the no-kissing rule, she was going to have a hell of a job enforcing it. She had to keep her focus—*their* focus—purely on sex. Which was not to be confused with pure sex. "I'll believe it. I've already seen it, remember?" She gave him an over-the-jeans cock stroke, in case he didn't. "Doesn't mean I'm not up for seconds, though."

The flare of his pupils said he hadn't forgotten. He caught her hand and pressed it against the denim-clad ridge of his dick. "I didn't bring the car into town because I planned to have a drink. How fast can you walk?"

"How far?" Her voice hitched with breathlessness, and the warm, liquid feeling between her thighs made it hard to stand, never mind walk. Excitement bubbled through her. Soon, very soon, she'd get what she'd been dreaming of. What *true* fantasies were about.

Erik jerked his head toward the northern end of the beach. "Five clicks."

She stared in that direction, as though she could make out the pinpricks of light. "The Point?" He didn't dress like anyone from The Point. Despite only being in the area for a couple of weeks, she'd have been willing to bet no one from there had a job. Well, the chauffeurs and housekeepers worked, but probably not the homeowners.

"My brother and I split an apartment there." Erik said, as though that explained how they could afford the location. "And a place out of town, so we're not in each other's hair."

"Five kilometers will take an hour. I'll get my car."

Chapter Five

She drove like a maniac. Which shouldn't surprise him, given her attitude. She'd been holding her own against the intimidation of those idiots at the café and hadn't seemed thrilled at his intervention. Considering the stinging slap she'd laid on the werewolf-faced jerk, she hadn't needed his help, but testosterone had kicked in the moment he saw her, the threat of competition tightening his balls. And not in a good way.

He gripped the armrest as the car cornered. Shame the bastards had backed away from a fight. He wouldn't have minded an excuse to pummel them into the ground, even though they'd only been after the same thing he wanted. Difference was, like all Mer, he'd seek permission, not make half-assed, drunken advances. The Mer men were all over the fact that nothing was sexier than a woman's full, informed consent. Well, they kind of had to be. Poseidon's not-so-enlightened ways had left them with a lot of ground to make up.

He unlocked his apartment, the woman right behind him. Her short breaths either indicated she was incredibly unfit, panting from the four shallow steps up to the front door, or she was as horny as he was. With any other woman, he wouldn't have thought that possible, but considering the way she'd acted in the ocean a couple of days earlier... Gods, he was glad he'd found her again. Though he'd had shifts at the lifeguard station, disappointed when she hadn't shown up there, and a bit of internet searching to do at Daniel's behest, trying to trace the parent company of the *Poseidon's Nemesis* and cohort, he'd spent more than a reasonable amount of time strolling the beach, foreshore, and town. Totally not looking for her.

As he turned to close the door behind her, she crowded into his space, dropping her bag, hand unerringly going for the bulge in his jeans.

"I want this. Now."

Fuck. She definitely wasn't one to mince words. He grabbed her waist and pulled her close, biting at her neck. She'd made her aversion to kissing clear, but dammit, foreplay always started with kissing. She was throwing him off his stride.

Not that his dick seemed to realize that.

His hands slid under the hem of her short skirt and over the rounding of her small, tight butt.

Pushing closer, she forced him back, one knee jammed against the wall so she could grind her pelvis against his thigh. Her hands were under his shirt. "Off. I want this off."

"Awkward, given that I don't want to let go of this." He squeezed a handful of her ass.

She snatched the bottom of his shirt and jerked it above his pecs, then hooked her tongue through his nipple ring, tugging on it. Hell, no woman had ever done that, and he wasn't prepared for the jolt of lust it shot to his balls, his cock jerking up like it was attached by an invisible chain.

He yanked his shirt off, grabbed her waist, and lifted her onto the narrow hall table, sweeping aside the fruit bowl and keys with his forearm. Her skirt bunched high around her smooth thighs, he positioned himself between her legs so his denim-clad cock ground against her pussy. Her musk filled the room, and Gods, he needed to taste her.

"Your knees," she gasped, the words coming out an odd mix of pleading and command.

"Yeah, there was some talk about that, right?" he teased. He'd give her what she wanted, all right. But not quite how she expected it, because he knew how to make it better. How to keep her begging for more.

She flashed a grin. "Way too much talk, I'd say. Not enough action."

"You're ready for some action, then? You're in the driver's seat." He seized her hips, pulling her to the edge of the table, and dropped to his haunches. Plunged his face between her thighs, biting at her plump mound.

"Oh!" she gasped, spreading her thighs farther apart. "Oh, yes!"

His tongue traced her swollen pussy lips through her underwear, the mounds and valleys of her sex outlined through the sodden fabric. "Like this?" he said, his mouth pressed to her cleft, dropping his voice low so it'd vibrate through her. "Or this?" He angled so his chin drove deep into her as his teeth found her clit through the material, nipping at the hard nub.

"That, yes, that. All of that," she panted. The wooden bench banged against the wall as she humped his face. One of her hands gripped the beveled edge of the table, her knuckles tiny white cockleshells as she forced herself up to meet his mouth. The other found the back of his head, urging him closer. "You're going to make me come, and I haven't got my pants off yet."

He couldn't hold in his chuckle at her aggrieved

tone. "Plenty of time. You said you were up for seconds, remember? Or I could just back off, if you prefer?"

"Don't you dare," she snarled, her hand winding tighter in his hair. "I want you to make me come. I want to know what it's like."

What it was like? Had she never...? No, that wasn't possible. But stupidly, he had to know. He drew back a little, his finger stroking her slit through her panties. "You mean you've never had an orgasm?"

She made a frustrated noise deep in her throat. "Of *course* I have." She glanced down and scowled as she caught him watching her. "Jeez. Well, if you have to know, just never like...this. Y'know." She hunched her shoulder and gestured with her chin toward him kneeling between her legs.

"You've never gotten off with oral?" He did like a challenge.

He couldn't pull his gaze from the tug of her white teeth on the pouted, reddened flesh as she worried at her lip. Eyes closed, she blew out an exasperated breath. "I've never had oral. Okay?"

"But you're so damn good at it."

A smile quirked her lips, though her eyes didn't reflect the emotion. "Didn't say I never *gave* it. Just that my partner wasn't big on the whole notion of reciprocity. Particularly when it came to something he figured was perverted."

Hell, he liked the idea of virgin territory even more than he liked a challenge. "He reckons oral's perverted? Then we're not doing it like this."

Disappointment tightened her face, but he stood, pulling her close so her legs reflexively wrapped his hips. He scooped her up and strode toward his wing of the house.

While her lips nuzzled his neck, he murmured in her hair, "I'm going to lay you on my bed and spread your legs wide open so I can admire your pretty little pussy. I plan to lick every sweet inch of your tight snatch, eat it out, show it all the attention it's never had. And then I'm going to tongue fuck you. Do you know what I want in return?"

She shook her head.

"I want you to come on my tongue, coat my face with your honey, so I can lap it all up. It's the least I can do as payback for the most awesome blowjob I've had in my life. Deal?"

"Deal," she whispered.

He lay her on the king-size bed and stood back. Took a hell of a lot of deep breaths. Though he spent a lifetime searching for women who'd consent to a ménage so he wouldn't endanger his immortality, he'd never taken a virgin because she wouldn't fully understand what she consented to. Not that this woman was claiming to be that rare unicorn, of course. But damn close. Experienced enough to know—and demand—what she wanted, but a virgin when it came to an oral orgasm. Which meant he could provide her something she'd never had.

And that was fucking unbelievably awesome.

Unless he couldn't get her to come?

A glance at the woman on the bed shoved aside the unfamiliar performance anxiety. Hells, she'd proved at the beach how wild she was, how wanton. She'd come, all right, even if he had to spend hours finding the right buttons to push.

What better way to spend a night?

She sat up, pulling off her shirt and unclasping her bra with a businesslike air. He almost wanted to tell her to wait, to let him unwrap his own present, but he detected a degree of nervousness, as though she'd set her mind on a course and was determined to follow it through. He stopped her when she lay back and hooked her thumbs in the sides of her panties, though. "Let me?"

She nodded but grabbed his wrist as he knelt beside her, his hands on her cotton underwear. "Wait. The rules."

"Safe word, you mean?" Not really necessary for what he had planned. BDSM had never been his thing.

She shook her head, sun-streaked hair spread in layers of gold and silver across the pillow. He tried to keep his eyes on her face, not on the jostle of her pert breasts, the nipples hard and rosy and begging for his mouth.

"No. Rules. I'm not into...well, no kissing, you already know that. And no, well, no P in the V, okay?"

"No intercourse, you mean? Perfect." At least, it should be, considering that was the one thing he couldn't give her. Not until Jax was there. So why, now, did he have such an urge to plunge his cock into her? He repeated her rule, as though it'd cement the fact in his own mind. "Sex is off the table."

"It is now that you carried me in here." She angled her head toward the table they'd just abused in the entry hall. "But yeah. No table, or anywhere else. I like you, but I don't want anything...serious. Regular sex is too much like..." Her thumb and finger clicked together as she hunted for words.

His heart jolted like he'd been hit with a stingray's barb. "Too much like…bonding?"

"Exactly!" Delight lit her face, and she sat up.

Gods, how was it possible? Didn't he know all the Mer this side of the equator? Yet she was definitely Mer, and like him, trapped in the search for sex that wouldn't cost her immortality. Unless…

He stroked his thumb over her palm. "Sex is only an issue if we have a monogamous thing going on, though, right? A ménage would change the dynamic, stop the relationship becoming…serious." Or fatal. Though only if one of them was human.

She dropped her chin, avoiding his gaze. "Um. I guess so. Maybe. Potentially. I mean, it's not like monogamy is a natural state, is it?"

He winced. No Mer would sound so doubtful about a fact they'd understood to be true for hundreds of years. Well, none except Trent and Jayde, maybe, who seemed well on their way to adopting human rules. He frowned at her hand. All Mer had large hands, a physical adaptation for deploying the webbing between their fingers. Though perfectly formed, her hands were, like the rest of her, petite.

"If we have regular sex, it's like…" She shrugged. "I don't know, it's only one step away from spooning, going for turmeric lattes on a Sunday morning, and discussing what towels to buy as we thumb through the real estate pages. It's like a form of commitment. This"—she waved a hand through the charged air between them—"what we're doing, this is hot and fun. Let's keep it like that."

His heart plummeted, which made no damn sense, as he had no reason to want her to be Mer. He just wanted to get her off.

Didn't he?

The fact she was human made for only a slight inconvenience, a delay until Jax arrived.

She curled her legs beneath her, kneeling so she was eye level with him, her tone earnest. "It's just that regular intercourse screws everything up, y'know?"

Nope. It was amazing just how much he did *not* know, given his age.

Her words filtered through to his brain. She'd made a point of using and emphasizing certain terms. *Intercourse. P in the V. Regular sex.*

She wasn't forbidding him, so much as she was telling him what *was* on the table. His nostrils flared, drinking in the intoxicating scent of her lust. The promise was in what she *wasn't* saying. He grinned. "Game on. Your rules, you're in charge."

She took his face between her hands, her pert nipples pressed against his chest. "You have no idea how hot that is."

For a moment he thought she'd break the rules and kiss him, but at the last second, she changed her angle of attack and rasped her hot, wet mouth across his stubble, before finding his ear and darting her wicked little tongue in.

He grabbed her hips and lifted so she dropped back among the pillows with a squeal. "I seem to remember I was tasked with a mission." This woman had a knack for throwing him off balance, making him lose his focus. "First oral orgasm ever, right?" He cracked his knuckles and twisted his head from side to side, releasing his jaw like he was limbering up for a game.

"I believe that was the deal." She was sinking

between two of the huge pillows the housekeeper had plumped when she made up the bed.

He slid a hand beneath her head, lifting her to tuck a cushion behind her shoulders. "I want you to watch what I'm doing to you."

Her throat bobbed as she swallowed, her eyes as huge as an octopus's.

He leaned over her, supporting himself on his arms. Mindful of her rules, he kissed her cheek, brushing his lips over the light smatter of freckles, then along the line of her jaw to her chin. Took his time working his lips down the slender column of her neck to her throat. Her pulse beat frantic there, and he dipped his tongue into the delicate orange-blossom-scented hollow.

Her shaky exhale stirred his hair, and he grinned. She'd enjoy this so much more with the build of anticipation. He trailed one finger down her clavicle to the enticing cupcake of her breast. Her cherry nipples peaked, and his hand moved to one, tweaking as his lips found the other. If she wouldn't let him kiss her properly, he'd damn well work out his mouth everywhere else.

She moaned and arched her back.

He released her nipple to murmur, "You like?"

"I like," she sighed.

"Then you're going to love what's coming." His hand swooped across her flat stomach to the saturated scrap of fabric between her legs. Nothing was hornier than a girl with wet panties. He rasped his fingertips up and down the material, then lifted them to his lips, licking them dry.

Her gaze glued to his fingers.

"Normally I'd kiss you, share the taste. But I guess I get to be greedy this time," he said. Ridiculous how desperately he wanted to kiss her, knowing it was forbidden.

Her lips quirked, but he could read the tense anticipation in the rigid line of her body. She wanted this so badly she was primed to explode.

He moved down the bed, parting her legs and settling his shoulders between her thighs. "Watch." He took a long lick up her fabric-draped slit.

She whimpered.

Rewarding. The type of women he usually hung out with didn't generally get to whimpering so early on. At least, not genuinely.

Her breasts quivered like tiny jellies as her chest rose erratically, but she didn't take her eyes from him.

He edged her panties aside. Lowered his head, his tongue finding her exposed lips. "Gods. So smooth. So sweet." He intended to tease her by demanding she watch, but maintaining eye contact was torment for him, too. He wanted to view his prize.

He licked again, his eyelids heavy with desire. Then he traced a finger over the pouted flesh of her sex. Breathed against the wetness. She trembled. "You are so gorgeous. Spread your legs wider. I want to see all of you."

She complied instantly, shifting higher on the pillow, her face and chest already flushed. She was into it. His problem wouldn't be making her come; it would be holding her back from coming too soon. What sort of idiot had she been with, that he'd willingly miss out on this?

Erik hid an exultant smile with another long lick.

Not deep, not yet. His cock pulsed as the folds that protected her core swelled, glistening with his saliva and her excitement. Frustration darted through him. His dick was never going there, not unless she decided she was into Jax as well as him.

He clambered to his knees and shifted to one side of the bed. She looked suddenly wary, as though she expected him to run. He shook his head. "I want these off." He drew her panties down her hips. "I don't want anything between my fingers, my mouth, my tongue, and your hot little slit."

As she nodded, her long blonde hair spilled over her face. He reached up and smoothed it aside. "And I want to see your face when you come. I want to see you and hear you and *taste* you, okay?"

She didn't reply, probably because her breaths were so ragged she couldn't.

He settled between her thighs again, stroking the exposed folds. "Gods, you have a pretty pussy." He pinched her swollen lips closed and trailed his tongue along her slit, tasting her essence, a honey-thick mixture of salt and vanilla.

Her clit stood proud, engorged with desire. He flicked it with his tongue, rewarded by her moan. Burying his chin deep into her, he sucked the hard nub into his mouth, grazing it with his teeth.

Her hands slammed into the bedcover either side of her hips as she gasped.

He lifted his head, his chin dripping with the evidence of her lust. Slid his finger down her slit. "Deeper?"

She nodded.

Two fingers this time, tracing but never entering.

"Deeper?"

She fisted the cover in her hands and nodded again.

This time, he slid one finger all the way inside her, his knuckles pressed into her wet channel.

Eyes closed, she arched her hips, biting her lip as she held back her orgasm.

She had to be kidding. One finger and she'd give it to him?

Fuck, he had to have her.

"Give me your hands." When she didn't comply, seeming unable to unlock her grasp on the linen, he took her hands and placed them on her labia. "Spread yourself open for me. I want to see everything. I want to fuck you." She tensed, and he continued smoothly, "With my tongue. I'm going to make you come, remember? I'm going to fuck your tight little hole with my fingers and my tongue, and you're going to drench me with your sweet juice."

Her fingers slid in her own slickness, trying to find purchase, but she spread her legs wider. He moved his hands under her butt, lifting her to his mouth. Licked deep and long, laving her slit.

She whimpered and panted, her thighs quivering on either side of his face.

He could sense how close she was, her back a strung bow, her feet dug into the mattress. He wouldn't need his fingers to get her off, but damn, he wanted to have something inside her.

He plunged his tongue deep, straight into her liquid core, and she gasped, her juices flooding his mouth. But still, she wasn't quite there. Holding her buttocks so she was captive against his mouth, he traced the crack of her ass with his finger as his tongue delved deeper and faster. Her thighs clamped around his head as his searching finger found the furled bud, dripping with her excitement. Jaw aching, he thrust his tongue as far and fast and hard as he could reach, and at the same moment, pressed his finger against the tight pucker of her ass.

It tipped her over the edge. Hips bucking to meet his mouth, she wrapped her hands in his hair, forcing his face into her slit as though he could possibly get any closer, any deeper.

Gods, sweet, she tasted so sweet.

He licked and sucked greedily, sweeping his tongue from her clit right down to her ass, teasing at the edge of the sensitive muscle, and then plunging deep into her velvet snatch as she shuddered and moaned.

"Oh, God, that was amazing." Her words jerky, she collapsed in a quiver of naked, primed, slick, wet desirability in the center of his bed.

So he did the only thing a decent Mer could do; he pushed himself from the bed, retrieving his shirt and pulling it back on.

She shoved upright. "Where are you going?"

Concern laced her voice. She was worried she'd done something to drive him away. Had her boyfriend's fucked morality screwed her up that bad?

He crossed to the robe and pulled a clean button-through shirt from a hanger. Handed it to her with a grin. "If I stay here, sweetheart, I'm about to get in all kinds of trouble with your rules. Plus, I got kind of sidetracked, but I do have other pussies I need to take care of."

Crap, that joke was about Trent's level, not his. But there was no blood in his brain, it'd all gone to his aching cock.

He retained his grip on the shirt as she reached for it. Maybe he should change his mind? This woman would probably have no issue with him beating one out over her cute ass. Fists clenched, his nostrils flared as he imagined the seed that swelled his balls spraying across the rounded cheeks of her butt.

Gods, he wanted to get off on her.

Problem was, he couldn't trust himself to keep it at that. Not right now.

He let go of the shirt.

She pulled the white top over her head and stood. The fabric fell to mid-thigh, the minimal covering possibly even sexier than her nakedness. Her breasts punched tiny mountains against the material, and he brushed his thumb over her nipple.

She sucked in a quick breath. "So pussy. Either you took my suggestion about non-monogamy instantly to heart, or you have a cat?"

"Does it matter which?"

"Not really." She shrugged, crossing her arms over her chest, the gesture at odds with her nonchalant words.

"In that case, I don't have a cat. Come on, I'll introduce you."

She hung back for a moment, and he wondered if she'd refuse, if jealousy would seize her. Why the heck did he want it to? Avoiding jealous women went hand in hand with never learning their names—yet he was having a hellish time not asking hers. He'd called her sweetheart, but the second the word was out of his mouth it'd seemed almost…derogatory. Maybe because he'd used it so many times before, for so many faceless women.

He shook the thought away and led her through the large apartment, her footsteps almost soundless behind him. He could smell the scent of sex, taste her sweet saltiness at the back of his throat. Even if he couldn't get his rocks off, he'd happily give her another orgasm, right now.

They traversed a hall, her steps slowing as she examined the huge canvases lining the gallery, photographs of corals and anemones, seahorses and jellyfish in all their vibrant, otherworldly colors. Three steps down into his sunken lounge room, furnished in chrome and leather, then up into another long, tiled gallery. At the far end of that hall, he cracked the door, peering around it before he opened it wide. As usual, the menagerie burst into action, racing toward him with yips and yowls.

He caressed the wolfhound's ears. "Some guard dog you are, Atlas." He glanced at the woman. "He's supposedly deaf, but I reckon it's selective. Seems to hear his biscuits hitting the bowl well enough."

She offered her palm to the dog, her grin widening. "Oh, you do have cats."

"Yeah, you thought being owned by one made you a crazy cat lady? I have five. And Atlas, who's so messed up he probably thinks he's a cat."

She moved farther into the room and bent to encourage a Russian Blue, who feigned disinterest.

The maneuver almost exposed her ass beneath the tail of his button-through, and definitely exposed the trails still glossy on her thighs. *Fuuuuck.* Where the hell was Jax? He couldn't hold out much longer. Not unless she was willing to let him try some other stuff.

"Five? Wow. A man of many excesses, huh?"

He dragged his gaze to her face as she looked at him over her shoulder, the haughty Russian Blue now rubbing against her hand. *Damn.* She totally realized he'd been checking out her ass, but still she didn't straighten, challenging him to keep his eyes on her face. She was fucking with both his mind and his self-control.

"Uh. Yeah. Rescues. In another life I was—would like to be—a vet." Still she didn't straighten. Gods, he couldn't fuck her, no matter what. But if she'd just let him kiss her— "That one's Sasha." He pointed at the blue. "And Acid." He gestured toward a calico sitting on the windowsill, her tail twitching as she eyed them.

"Acid? Hardly a warm, fuzzy name."

"I'm more than happy to note that not all pussies are fuzzy." He waited for the flare of realization in her eyes. "Though I don't have a Sphinx. Acid is named for her eyes. Looks like she's been tripping." As though she knew what he was saying, the cat turned her permanently startled gaze on him.

The woman nodded, straightening—thank the Gods—and stalked the few steps back to him. "A guy who's into animals is kind of a turn on."

He chuckled. "You might want to replay that in your head."

She wrinkled her nose. "Ugh. I meant I could get right into a guy who really likes pussies."

"In that case, I could definitely get right into pussies."

"You already did." She pressed her near naked body against his. "And I want more."

"But you said no—"

She angled her head toward the bedroom. "Back there, you did something I liked."

"Only one thing? Disappointing."

She took his hand and placed it on her ass. His fingers slid into the cleft of her buttocks. "Back…there, I mean."

He slipped his hand beneath the shirt tail, his fingertips lightly circling, teasing her tantalizingly tight entrance. "Like, right here?"

"Uh huh," she said, but he didn't miss the anxious flicker that crossed her face, her quick intake of breath.

He reached to drift his finger through her thick juices, then returned to circle the taboo opening. Desire flared in her eyes. "So you're into this?"

She lifted one shoulder, doing that damn thing with her teeth on her lip again.

"It's something else you've never tried, then?"

Another shrug. That, along with her breathless tension as she leaned into him, indicated a definite yes.

His finger probed the tight rosebud, his cock literally dripping as she flinched. If she carried on looking at him like that, all doe-eyed trust and longing, fear mixed with excitement, he was going to kiss her.

Instead, he cupped her butt tighter, pulling her hard against his cock. Pressed the pad of his lubricated finger against her exquisitely unyielding back passage. "For your first time, you need to be almost ready to come before I give it to you. You need to be begging for it so when I feed my cock into this tight little hole, you come instantly. Because you won't want more than a second or two of me inside you. Not until you learn how to…accommodate…me."

"That's not what it looked like when I researched

it."

He tried not to laugh at the irritation in her tone, as though he'd mansplained something she'd already analyzed. "I'll bet your research was conducted on sites designed for men's pleasure. What we like and what you can take are sometimes kind of at opposite ends of the scale. And I'm more interested in giving you pleasure than imitating a porn star."

Fine words, but damn, the thought of her fingers frigging her hot little clit as she "researched" sexual taboos was almost enough to drive him over the edge.

One day, he'd pound his cock into her tight little ass.

But not today.

Chapter Six

Erik stiffened, his head tilted to one side, as though he listened to something.

Not that he'd be able to hear a thing over her breathing. His arm wrapped around her, holding her captive against his hard abs, he had his finger in her ass.

God. Actually *in* her ass. Not patting her butt or playing with her bum or squeezing her cheeks. His finger was in her hole, pulsing as he warned that she had to be ready to come before he'd go any farther. Couldn't he tell that his words alone had her ready to go? Again.

Suggesting to Brandon—after years of barely-even-vanilla sex—they experiment with anal had been a deal breaker. He'd been adamant that only sluts and hookers ever allowed backdoor visits, and that her desire proved she wasn't wife material.

Maybe not so much a deal breaker as a lifesaver, then. She almost giggled; here she was, with another lifesaver, who was telling her exactly how he planned to fuck her ass.

Erik looked down at her, the left side of his mouth lifting.

Why did she want to know how that mouth tasted? Why did the idea of kissing him while his fingers stroked inside her turn her on so much? Kissing was nothing more than a dutiful greeting and farewell, a dry press of chaste lips, which once a fortnight evolved into a wet exchange of germ-laden spit that seemed designed to prove ownership.

Brandon had not been a good kisser.

But maybe she wasn't either.

Erik stroked slightly roughened fingertips down her cheek. "You remember I said I have a mate coming over? He'll be here in five. Do you want to…meet…him?"

Considering her insinuation at the café and his mention of ménages, she knew exactly what he meant.

And that was both exciting and terrifying. Because he'd been right, when he clarified her rules; if there were three of them in the…relationship…neither of the guys would claim ownership. Plus, if they were into that level of kink, they wouldn't judge her for the things she wanted to try.

Not that Erik seemed disposed to judge her.

"Sure." She almost swallowed the word.

He kissed her cheek and gave her bottom a light slap. "I have to feed this lot. Scat's been nibbling on my toe for the last five minutes."

She glanced down. He wasn't joking. A black and white cat flopped across his feet, rasping his toes with a sandpapery tongue. A tatty-eared marmalade cat sat nearby, while the Russian Blue glared judgmentally. At her, not the other cats. And now she felt kind of embarrassed, making out under their scrutiny. She shifted away from Erik. "I thought you said five cats?"

"Midge is blind. And ridiculously old. Her owner went into a care facility, and they directed her to have Midge euthanized. So"—he lifted an open hand, signifying that the result was a foregone conclusion—

"she ended up here. She has a room next door, as this lot tend to bowl her over."

"Your cat has its own bedroom?" At The Point?

"Yeah. She's happier that way. Twice a week I take her to the rest home to visit Dulcie. I'm not sure Dulcie recognizes her anymore, but I figure it can't hurt, right? And Midge likes the trip out, getting the wind in her fur."

"I thought cats hated being in cars?"

Erik bent to push the cat off his foot, scratching its belly. "Luckily, Midge doesn't. Though I don't actually have the top down—I wouldn't fancy driving a couple of hours each way with a yowling cat. She does insist on choosing the music, though."

"A couple of hours? That's eight hours a week." Plus the actual visit time, however long it took a blind cat and senile old woman to re-bond.

He shrugged. "It's only time. Doesn't cost me anything."

She jerked her chin at the door into the next room. "Except for providing private bedrooms for cats."

"And that's only money. Scraps of paper with a completely arbitrary nominal value." He grinned. "Plenty of time to make more scraps of paper."

Only someone wealthy would ever think like that. Working for a not-for-profit was more about passion than pay, but it didn't afford her the luxury of being oblivious to the state of her finances.

Erik pointed behind her, in the approximate direction of the front door, not that she'd been paying much attention to her environs. "Jax is on his through the compound gate."

She glanced around the room for a CCTV screen.

"How do you know?"

"Ah." Erik rubbed one hand along his shadowed jaw. "We're cousins. So y'know, that kind of blood link thing, I guess." He tapped his temple.

Obviously, he heard the car or something, though the throaty, yearning blues playing throughout the house on some invisible sound system was all she could pinpoint. "Can I, uh, grab a shower?"

"Course. Back through my room. There are fresh towels in the en suite. Would you like your back scrubbed?" He ran his fingertips down the center of her spine, raising a delicious trail of goosebumps. "Offer isn't location specific."

Her nostrils flared as she hunted for oxygen, suddenly short in the large room. "I'd take you up on it, but..." This time she gestured toward the door as a melodic chime sounded.

Erik pressed closer. "It's a very large shower."

She shook her head. Chicken. "And you're a very large guy." Would his cousin be as huge? God, was she seriously considering having both of them? "I won't be long."

Trepidation and excitement pounded through her veins as she sluiced water over her body. Erik hadn't been joking; the shower was the size of a small bathroom, with three shower heads, each set at a different height on opposing walls. What sort of orgies was he into?

More importantly, what sort of an orgy was she about to get into? Though a threesome wasn't an orgy, right? Still, she needed to decide whether she was in, or if it'd be a better plan to grab her keys from the hall table—*that* hall table—and run for it.

She dried off and retrieved her skirt and blouse from the floor, fumbling the buttons closed. Then she wandered through the apartment, the plush bedroom carpet giving way to cool white tiles, as she followed the masculine voices back to the sunken lounge in the center of the spacious house.

She paused in the arched entryway. This cousin—Jax—was almost as broad-shouldered as Erik. Which was great for making her feel delicate, but didn't do much for her courage.

In an oddly old-fashioned gesture, he rose from the leather lounge as she entered. He was naked except for shorts, and their build was the only similarity the cousins shared. Where Erik was dark, almost Mediterranean in hair and skin coloring, Jax was Nordic. A Viking god. His hair was caught in an untidy bun, and a trim beard outlined the hard cut of his jaw.

Erik also stood. "This is Jax. Who took so long to get here I was beginning to think he got lost."

"Sorry, cuz. The old man stopped me for the safe sex talk. Guess we're never too old, huh?"

Erik snorted. "Trent's probably got him worried. Lecturing him did me no good, but then it wasn't his upstairs head doing the thinking."

"True enough. He's got some more stuff for you to chase up, too, before the Council meeting."

Erik nodded, dismissing whatever work-related stuff Jax dragged up. "I'll organize some drinks. Wine or beer?"

Krissy dragged her gaze away from Jax. "Do you have juice, or something soft?"

"No alcohol?"

"Clear head, no regrets." Not that she was going to

have any, either way, but it wouldn't be a great idea to show for work with a hangover her first month at the new office.

"Good plan. I'll be back in a second," Erik said, one hand up, palm out. She got a clear *don't start without me* vibe.

Jax patted the seat beside him as he sat. "Sorry, I didn't catch your name."

He couldn't have, because Erik didn't know it. Which had been cool as part of her strategic maneuver on the beach, but now seemed a little odd, given her intentions. "Krissy."

The blond god took her hand in a loose, informal handshake. Except for his thumb stroking her knuckles. "Erik said you guys only just met?"

She dropped onto the seat, aided by shaky knees, and burrowed her toes into the luxurious, shaggy pile of the white rug. Jax had her name, and as she intended for him to have a whole lot more than that, he might as well have the full story. "Several orgasms ago." She pursed her lips to blow out a tense breath, hoping he wouldn't notice. She'd made a good call on the booze; this new, outrageous version of herself, equal parts exhilarating and terrifying, had zero need for alcoholic encouragement.

Jax flashed a grin. "Erik did mention something about you blowing his mind. I figured it for a metaphor."

"Dude, no metaphor." Erik set drinks on the glass-topped table. "She totally blew my mind. Just happened to be along with other parts of my anatomy." He handed her a juice. "Best keep your hydration up."

As he quirked an eyebrow, she kind of gurgle-snorted. But that may have been because Jax's hand landed on her thigh. She sipped the tart juice, barely able to swallow.

Jax's fingers brushed beneath the hem of her skirt, and he leaned in closer, the crisp scent of fresh ocean washing over her. "So—"

"Rules," Erik reminded.

Oh. Yeah. Right. She wasn't very good at the business side of this business. Heart racing, blood pounding in her ears, she'd damn near forgotten that deal. "Yeah, rules," she gasped, nodding at Erik. Hopefully, he'd detail them, as her brain was incapable of focusing on rules or limits or restrictions, or anything except the hot hand working up her thigh and the two men only inches from her.

Two gorgeous men, discussing having sex with her.

"No kissing." Erik flicked up a finger, as though he had a list to work through.

"Shame," Jax murmured, his knuckles against her chin as his thumb brushed her lips. His breath stirred her hair, and she could barely drag her eyes from the clean-cut bow of his lips. What would it be like to press her mouth against his, to taste his tongue, his desire?

Her own lips parted—God, she was practically panting—she forced herself to drop her gaze. To where a dragon coiled around Jax's arm like the figurehead on a Viking ship's prow, the forked tongue lashing across his sculpted pecs.

Great. More tongues. How was a girl supposed to remember her boundaries? And who could have known that the unspoken promise in a brief touch could be more tantalizing than the hottest kiss?

Except, maybe it wasn't. Perhaps a kiss could offer even more.

She didn't need experience to figure that making out with these guys would be nothing like kissing Brandon. What she *did* need was to rescind her own ridiculous no-kissing decree the second she could force her mouth to work like a normal human being's.

"And firsts are all mine," Erik continued.

She neither remembered that rule nor knew what it meant.

The cousins swapped a long, silent look, then Jax nodded. "Fair enough, bro. Happy to fit in."

His ice-floe blue eyes met hers, and he brushed his thumb across his own lips, then touched it to hers again, as though he was transferring an illicit kiss. She flicked the tip of her tongue over his thumb.

His pupils flared. "*Really* happy to fit in," he growled. "But that doesn't mean I'm not going to try to persuade you to change your mind."

"*Persuade* being the operative word. The choice is always yours," Erik said as he sat on the other side of her, rescuing the glass from her loose grasp and placing it back on the table. "We have a firm rule about consent."

We? Who, him and Jax? Somehow it didn't seem that was what he meant. Damn, if Brandon could see her now, he'd have a fit. Or insist she head off to his church to be exorcised, flogged, or doused in holy water. Possibly all of the above.

Well, tough shit, Brandon. She was wet enough without holy water, more into exercising with these guys than exorcising, and watching them flog off over her naked body was the only kind of flogging she intended to entertain.

She swiveled toward Erik, her knee brushing his thigh. "*You* can kiss me. You've earned the right."

A quick intake of breath swelled his chest. "So the hidden price was a certain number of orgasms?"

Jax whistled low. "Sweet idea. How many? I want in on that."

She started to answer, but Erik's fingers caught her chin, turning her back to face him. "Secret. You work on that, dude, while I claim my prize."

As Erik leaned in, she closed her eyes. Tried to remember how to breathe when kissing. A big breath now and hold it in? Or pant and hope he didn't notice? God, this was hopeless. She didn't know how to— His lips touched hers, a gentle meeting of sensitive flesh. At the same moment, Jax's hand swept beneath her skirt, encountering no barrier. Because, not only had her panties been wringing wet, but why play coy? Why pretend this wasn't what she wanted by putting underwear on?

She gasped as Jax's finger skimmed her swollen cleft. "Gods, so smooth," he murmured.

Erik's tongue slipped between her open lips, caressing hers, tangling and tasting, both men exploring her with assured, deft movements, the overwhelming sensations rolling one on top of the other.

Erik cradled the back of her head, plunging his tongue deeper. At the same instant, Jax's finger delved inside her, the timing perfect, as though the lifeguards somehow synchronized their moves.

She moaned, opening her mouth to Erik, parting her legs for Jax.

Jax dropped to his knees, pulling her hips to the

edge of the lounge. "Spread your legs for me, Krissy," he murmured. "Let me see."

She wanted to watch him, the blond head between her thighs, his shoulders forcing her knees wide, but Erik claimed her mouth, probing and searching with his tongue, one hand under her shirt, his thumb and forefinger tweaking her nipple as electric shocks of desire pulsed through her.

"Gods," he growled. "You have no idea how much I wanted to kiss you." He smiled against her mouth. "Actually, *I* had no idea how much I wanted to kiss you. But now I don't know what tastes sweeter. This"—he tangled his tongue with hers, darting it across her teeth, their breath mingling—"or this." His hand left her breast, sweeping down, skirting the bunched fabric of her sarong. His finger found her clit, rubbing with the perfect firm, circular motion.

As Jax buried his tongue deep in her pussy, fucking her with it.

Jesus.

She couldn't breathe.

Didn't want to breathe.

Didn't want to do a single thing that might interrupt this moment.

Erik slid his fingers down her slit, then brought them back up to his lips. Licked them, and then kissed her again, dipping his tongue into her mouth. He drew back. "I told you I like to share. Do you like that? Do you like the taste?"

She nodded.

He grinned in exultation, pinning her with his eyes. "Jax. Man. Swap."

Jax groaned, but as he stood she leaned forward,

settling her hand over the bulge in his pants. She wasn't a bystander; this was her fantasy. "I want to see."

Jax's hands went straight to his fly. Unbuttoned and dropped his shorts. Like Erik, he must spend a lot of time naked, his even tan honey-gold, rather than olive. He knelt alongside her on the lounge as Erik dropped between her legs. As her fist closed around Jax's rigid shaft, Erik nestled his chin in the apex of her thighs, grinning wolfishly at her. "Are you going to come for me again, Krissy?"

Somehow, hearing him say her name for the first time was a turn-on.

Ah, who was she kidding? Everything this guy did turned her on.

"Are you going to make me come?" she challenged. Though maybe the words weren't only for him. She'd had more orgasms in the last few hours than in the last few weeks. Was she capable of another?

"I'll do my best."

"Which has proven pretty satisfactory, so far," she said.

"Challenge accepted." Erik's dark head dipped between her thighs, the first touch of his tongue bringing a moan to her lips. Her fist tightened on the hard length of Jax's golden cock, pumping him in response to her own increasing need.

Jax closed his hand over hers, smoothing her jerky, overeager tugging. He chuckled. "Slow down, sweetheart. We're not going anywhere. Hey, Erik, don't make her come, all right? Seems I need to earn my entrance"—his fingers traced across her lips, his pupils dark with desire—"here."

She flicked his finger with her tongue, then

released his cock from her sweating palm. "You misunderstood. You can have *entry*." She licked her lips insinuatingly. "You just can't *kiss* me."

The dragon's tongue lashed as Jax's chest rose. "Damn, Erik was right. You are wild, woman." Laying one arm along the back of the chair, he shifted so that she only needed to lean forward an inch to taste him.

To taunt him.

To control him.

She swept her tongue over the head of his cock, teasing the eye where salty drops of pre-cum glistened. Though she could still feel the warmth of Erik's breath on her swollen pussy, he'd stopped licking. No! Because she planned to blow Jax? She skewed so she could see him, Jax's cock balanced on the tip of her tongue. If Erik didn't want her to do it, would she pass up the opportunity?

No. This was her fantasy.

His stubble-darkened chin gleaming with her juice, Erik winked and then worked one finger inside her. "Do it," he commanded. He pulled his finger out. Sucked on it and then eased it back between her thighs, teasing her entrance. She mewled, and he grinned. "Is this what you want? Do you want me to finger fuck you?"

She took a breath and slid her lips over the head of Jax's engorged cock.

Erik thrust his finger into her. "Yeah. That's it. Fuck him, Krissy."

This guy was watching her give head to another guy, and not only was he into it, but he was getting her off at the same time? Whose life was this?

Her eyes watered as Jax's cock hit the back of her throat, and she fisted him to keep the penetration shallower, trying to relax her jaw. Erik's tongue laved her slit, then two fingers hooked within her as he worked her clit with his thumb. Her hips rocked with his rhythm, grinding against the friction he provided.

Jax's hand wound in her hair, and she cupped his balls with her free hand. He groaned. "Gods, your tongue is slicker than a sea serpent. Suck it, Krissy."

She moaned, arching her hips to allow Erik access as his tongue probed within her.

Suddenly, he withdrew.

Jax pulled free of her mouth and shifted away.

She flicked her eyes open. Stood between her splayed thighs, Erik leaned forward, his hands against the back of the lounge, either side of her shoulders. His words, murmured low and sexy, made her heart shudder to a halt. "Do you want to taste yourself, Krissy?" Without waiting for her response, he touched his lips to hers, deepening the kiss.

His tongue thrust into her mouth like it had in her pussy, and fingers—his, Jax's, who knew, who cared?—found her clit, massaging in quick, tight circles. She moaned and bucked her hips. Tore her mouth free of Erik's so she could protest on a snatched breath, "You're going to make me come."

Erik grinned. "That's kind of the game plan, here."

She shook her head. "No."

Instantly, both men stepped back, the hot press of their bodies replaced by cool air. Not quite what she'd had in mind.

"No?" Erik held up one palm to Jax, as though restraining him, but his raised eyebrow was for her.

She shook her head. "No. For one thing, you're still dressed."

"Easy fixed." He grabbed the neck of his shirt and ripped it over his head.

God, both men were seriously gorgeous. Like, unbelievably so. Ripped hard, but not over-muscled gym junkies. Perfect, flawless bodies, like the statue of David.

But with better hair.

And bigger dicks.

Much, much bigger dicks.

"What else?" Erik asked.

"More rules." She dipped her chin so her eyelashes hid her gaze. It was hard, admitting her insecurities. But if she didn't, how would she surmount them? "I need you to come as well." Damn, she hated using the word *need*. Brandon had always made her feel needy, as though her desire for foreplay, an orgasm, or variety was aberrant, an obligation that gave him no pleasure. That evidently wasn't the case with these guys, but still, she needed to explain. She licked her lips. "If you just keep getting me off, it's kind of like…you're not really into me, y'know? You're doing me a favor."

"You're kidding, right?" Jax glanced at Erik, then frowned at her.

The muscles in Erik's shoulders bunched, and the leather near her head squeaked in protest at his grip as he loomed over her again. "I'd like to meet your ex. He has a lot to answer for." He sounded like he actually planned to confront Brandon.

Jax dropped between her knees, his breath hot against her center. He edged up the hem of her sarong, his thumb stroking her clit as he looked up at her, hunger stark in his eyes. "Damn, Krissy, I could get off hands-free, watching you come. You're fucking gorgeous." He took a swipe up her pussy with his tongue. "And you taste amazing."

She braced her hands against Erik's hard chest as his lips crashed into hers, demanding, devouring, plundering. As she gasped, his mouth traced along her jaw to her ear, and he nipped at her lobe, his ragged breath hot and harsh in her ear. "Krissy, you've no idea how much I want to fuck you. How badly I want to come inside you. Tell me I can."

Her fingertips caressed the sharp cut of his blue-black jaw. Erik tasted of her, and Jax's face was between her thighs. There'd never be another opportunity like this. She had to ask for what she wanted. No flowery euphemisms. "You know what we talked about before?"

Erik looked puzzled, lifting one shoulder. "Old people, cats, dogs, drinks…I'm lost."

She swallowed, her mouth impossibly dry. Unlike certain other parts. "A—" Nope, she couldn't do it. That particular word wasn't going to come easy— unlike her. So she'd permit one slightly floral euphemism. "Greek."

Chapter Seven

"Are you sure?" His heart hammered so hard there was a chance he'd miss her all-important reply. "You have to be certain because, right now, I don't have enough blood in my brain to do a convincing job of lying to you, Krissy. I can't pretend I don't want you like that. Like I don't want you every way you'll let me have you." And as many times as she'd let him, too, but it was best not to terrify her with that.

Or scare himself shitless, because since when did he want a woman for more than one night? Gods, Trent was rubbing off on him. Why the hell else would the notion of limiting himself to one woman after only a couple of hundred years of sampling pop into his head?

Just because she was funny, horny as hell, and sexier than anything he'd ever touched. And her name on his lips sounded like something illicit, something forbidden after decades of avoiding such intimacy. Though, with his hand wound into her hair, he could barely keep his lips off hers long enough to speak her name. Damn, what was with that? If she hadn't initially forbidden kissing, would he be so into it now? Maybe she was a shrink or something, because it sure seemed she knew how to play with his mind.

He shoved upright, running a hand through his hair, as though he could force order into his brain. At least he'd not been the one to ask her name. It wasn't like he'd broken his own rule. And of course, he probably didn't really want her for more than one night. Hell, they were only a few hours in, barely even started.

There was nothing for him to worry about.

Except that, if she said they needed to cool it for now, that she wanted to wait, he'd be asking to see her again.

Begging.

Pleading.

Fuck. He was in trouble.

"Wait" was not the sentiment coming from her perfect, reddened lips, though. She looked up at him, her chestnut eyes flashing with golden glints, like summer sunlight catching the ripples on the ocean. "You said I need to be ready. If I'm any more ready, I'll explode."

Jax leapt to his feet. "You're up for it? Excellent. Yeah, I heard you, dude." He held up a hand to forestall Erik's protest. "You claimed firsts. I take it this is a first?"

"Hell, yeah, this is a first." He had to be her first, because he needed to make sure she was treated right. He focused on his cousin, tapping him mentally. *Just take it easy on her, bro. Despite how it looks, she's not experienced. In anything.*

Jax offered a hand to Krissy, tugging her to her feet. "Hearing ya, dude. You lead and I shall follow."

Krissy frowned at him, then at Jax. Hearing only part of their conversation must make it sound odd.

He closed the space between them, his fingertips tracing the slender column of her throat as she swallowed nervously. He plucked at the neck of her blouse. "Seems you're the one who's overdressed now."

Something exploded far away, a dull roar that rattled the windows. All three of them reflexively glanced toward the door, but then Krissy gave a dismissive shrug, her fingers moving to her buttons.

"Let me." Jax flipped the buttons single-handed and slid the shirt from her shoulders, as Erik untangled the knot on her short sarong, leaving her naked before them.

"Niiiice," Jax breathed appreciatively. "Dad could be right. Maybe I do have a thing for seals." He ran his hand over Krissy's pert breasts. Her nipples peaked instantly, her stomach tensing as his hand swooped lower, his fingers spread to cover the mound of her pudenda. Her eyes widened, lips parting on a tiny moan, and Erik knew Jax had slipped a finger straight inside her slick pussy.

"Seals?" she gasped.

Jax shook his head. "Joke. I'm into gals, not gills. But I am into this. Smooth. So slippery. I need to taste again."

"Wait." Erik scooped her up in his arms and strode to the bedroom. He had very specific ideas of how this should play out. And it started with him getting his jeans off before he burst out of them.

He steadied her in the center of the room, then shucked his pants. Her nipples hot coals against his abs, he pulled her close and lowered his lips to hers. Her mouth opened beneath his, a sucking anemone, tasting and tangling as she gripped the back of his neck like she'd devour him.

As his hands roamed the gentle sway of her back, exploring the rounding of her bottom, she willowed toward him, pressing the apex of her legs against his thigh. Palming her ass, he squeezed, separating the cheeks. Jax moved in behind her, reaching around to pinch her swollen nipples.

Eyes closed, she thrust her breasts into Jax's hand, her butt curved out to meet his own caress. He slid his hands down the crack of her ass, his index finger teasing her tight rosebud.

She gasped, and her eyes flashed open.

"Slower?" He shifted his hands up to the small of her back. "I don't want to hurt you." There was a hell of a difference between her thinking she was ready and actually being able to take him.

She grasped the back of his neck, pulling his head down to hers. Pressed hard into her belly, his cock twitched and spasmed as she took his lip between her teeth, biting until he grunted in pain. She released the flesh, then slashed her hot, wet tongue over it, more tease than apology. "A little bit of pain's not always bad, right?"

He probed his lip with his tongue. "You're basing that on more untried research?" Damn, he'd like to put her over his knee for that stunt.

In fact, he would.

She pouted sympathetically, caressing his lip with her finger. "Absolutely. The internet's a wonderful tool. At least, it would be, if I was convinced that clearing my search history deleted all evidence."

Can I? Jax interrupted.

He focused on Jax's message. Damn. He wanted to say no, he wanted to keep all Krissy's firsts for himself. But he also wanted to see her face, didn't want to miss a second of her excitement, her reaction to the new experiences he and Jax could provide.

And it seemed most everything they could provide would be new, yet Krissy wasn't allowing fear to limit her need.

Go for it, he thought to Jax.

His cousin dropped to his knees behind Krissy. Even without the tantalizing mind images Jax flashed up to him, he knew the instant Jax's tongue pressed against Krissy's forbidden entrance, her mouth falling open in a perfect O, her shock immediately replaced by a desire he recognized as insatiable.

A hunger that could, perhaps, match his own.

Her pupils flared, then hid behind hooded eyelids as she pressed against him.

A muffled tone trilled, presumably from the depths of the bag she'd slung in the hall when they'd entered an orgasm or two ago, but Krissy didn't seem to notice.

"Spread your legs farther apart," he directed, prompted by Jax's silent message.

She complied instantly, and he slid his hand into her warmth, her thighs saturated with her dripping lust.

"Fuck," she moaned.

"All in good time." He grinned. "Begging for it, remember?" His fingers found her clit, and she bucked against his touch, grinding her taut stomach against his dick. He was leaking near as much as she was, his pre-cum leaving her belly slippery.

The phone cut out but immediately rang again. Krissy groaned, and he dropped to his knees, his mouth pressed to her slit, hands grasping her buttocks so Jax could work on her from behind.

Gods, this was perfect. If only the damn phone would stop ringing. He took a greedy swipe up Krissy's snatch, then leaned back to look up at her face. "Put your leg over my shoulder," he instructed.

Hands on his shoulders, she obeyed, revealing his glistening pink trophy. He slid one finger deep inside her. Soon, that would be his cock. Much as he wanted to fuck her ass, that wasn't the best place to start. Besides, he could do that when Jax wasn't around. When he didn't need to share. This pussy, though, this he could only have while Jax was here, the double pheromone load disrupting the DNA modification that sex with a Mer would cause in Krissy. And preserving his immortality.

Though that didn't seem so important, right now.

He only needed her permission. "Krissy, I want—"

The phone stopped and then rang again, an incessant demand. Krissy's hands stilled in his hair. She unhooked her leg from his shoulder, her long limbs lithe and supple. "Shit, has that been the same ringtone every time? I have to get it." She darted from the room, oblivious to the comedy in leaving him and Jax kneeling, facing each other.

Comedy was probably too strong a word. Without the buffer of a naked female body between them, the moment was awkward rather than funny.

Jax lifted one shoulder. "Well, I *thought* that was going well."

"Yeah, it was promis—"

Krissy's sharp gasp cut through his words. "What do you mean? When?" A pause. "Are you all right? I'll be there in five minutes."

She stumbled back into the room, clutching her cell phone. "That explosion? It was The Little Blue."

Chapter Eight

Even from the top end of the main street, a half kilometer away, the café flared like a candle with an untrimmed wick, competing with the flashing blue strobe of the local cop car and the red light of the rural fire service truck.

Krissy slammed her car into park and had the door open before the vehicle came to a standstill. Jax and Erik flanked her as she bailed from the car, scanning the small crowd congregated on the alfresco dining strip. Her chest eased a little at the sight of her boss, huddled with her arms crossed over her chest, beside a uniformed firefighter. Adele had obviously left home in a rush. Her hair, usually braided or plaited over one shoulder, fell thick and wavy to her waist, her feet bare and her usual uniform of peasant blouse and tie-dyed skirt replaced by baggy workout pants and a sweatshirt.

She turned as Krissy rushed toward her. "Oh, Krissy, you didn't need to come down, hon. I know you were…busy." Her eyes flitted toward Erik, widening as Jax took up station on the opposite side of her. "I only wanted to be sure that none of the staff were inside." She rubbed a hand across her furrowed brow, smearing a trace of soot beneath her bangs.

"What—?" Krissy coughed as a waft of acrid smoke caught her throat. "Do you know how the fire started?" She rarely had reason to be in the kitchen.

That was Adele's domain, but still, she mentally ran through her tasks, making certain she'd left nothing untended, nothing turned on.

"Probably too early to tell," the orange-clad firefighter offered.

"You're insured, Adele?" Erik asked.

The older woman nodded. "Yes. But you can bet it won't be enough, it never—"

"Adele!"

Adele flinched and swiveled to face the ocean as the male voice boomed from the esplanade. Three men strode toward them, each wearing the swim shorts that were part of the lifeguard uniform. Krissy frowned at the water carving furrows down their mostly naked bodies, pooling at their feet as they halted near Adele. Odd time of the night for a swim. Or more correctly, odd time of the morning, it had to be around two a.m. Maybe lifeguards up here did some weird kind of night-ops training, like the military. Nothing would get her into the ocean at night.

Erik's knuckles brushed her hip.

Yeah, okay, so there was *something* that might get her into the water.

The leader of the trio nodded a greeting to Erik, but spoke to Adele. "Are you all right? Was anyone hurt?"

Krissy recognized him. Not that she knew him, but she'd noticed him in the café a couple of times. He wasn't the kind of guy you could overlook. Actually, none of the men were. The youngest of them drew Jax to one side, and though he didn't appear to be speaking, Jax nodded his head in apparent agreement.

Erik caught her puzzled expression. "That's Tyson. Jax's brother."

As though that explained the nonverbal communication. Odd that she'd noticed Erik and Jax do the same thing.

Adele cut across her thoughts. "What on Earth are you doing here, Trent? Surely you can't see the flames from right out at The Point?"

"Ah, I wasn't there. Erik let me know there was a problem."

Krissy frowned. She and the guys had tugged their clothes on and rushed from the house. Erik must've texted while she drove. But how had Trent picked up the message when he'd been swimming?

Adele gestured toward the café, the flames already dying down under the high-pressure streams of water from the fire truck. "Everyone's accounted for. Poor Krissy here came rushing over, but the others are all home, safe."

Trent's eyes cut from Krissy to Erik to Jax. A slight smile played at the corner of his mouth as if he knew what they'd been up to.

The heat that engulfed her wasn't only from the flaming building.

Erik threaded his fingers through hers. "Krissy, my brother, Trent."

She flinched at his proprietorial grasp, then forced herself to relax. Any guy so keen to share her didn't have ownership issues. "Hi." She nodded at Trent. "Oh!" An explosion ripped through the side of the building, and they all startled. Erik's grip tightened, and Jax stepped up so that his body shielded her from the furnace blast.

Trent watched the flames for a moment. "Despite that heart-starter, it seems the firies have it under control. Sorry—" He reached for Krissy's hand, smirking as she disentangled herself from Erik. "Not sure I caught your name."

"You heard," Erik growled. "Krissy."

The brothers were like night and day, Erik all dark promise and sultry insinuation where Trent, his sun-streaked blond hair pulled into a ponytail, was an entirely palatable cross between Chris Hemsworth and Travis Fimmel. Not that she watched way too much TV.

Trent grinned at his brother, as though he'd scored a point. "Okay, then, if we're doing introductions…" He swept a hand wide to indicate the group. "My cousins, Jaxson and Tyson." He shot a glance at Krissy, his green eyes a shade darker than Erik's and dancing with fathomless mirth. "I'm sure you know at least a couple of these guys, Krissy, but Adele hasn't met them. And my uncle, Daniel."

If she'd been into older men—heck, if she hadn't been surrounded by hot guys—she'd totally have gone for Daniel's craggy silver-fox look. The guy knew how to rock debonair, despite dripping.

Except, he wasn't dripping. Hadn't the men been wet when they appeared, seconds ago? Yet as Daniel nodded a greeting, one hand running through his gray hair, there wasn't a drop of moisture on him.

She was probably the wettest one there.

She hid a snigger as a glance at Adele put the lie to that thought. Her boss flushed, her eyes bright as, distracted from her troubles, she wound an auburn ringlet around her finger. "Nice to meet you, Daniel."

"Dan," he suggested, his thumb smoothing the smudge of ash from her forehead. "Shame the circumstances aren't more pleasant. You weren't inside when the building went up, Adele?"

Adele paused for so long, Krissy considered jumping in to ease the conversation along. "I, uh, no. I was asleep." She pinched at her baggy top. "Sod's law. This had to happen the night my good pajamas are in the wash. I'll be plastered all over the local newspaper, looking like this."

"Really?" Deep furrows carved Daniel's cheeks. "What day does that come out? I'll make sure to pick up a few copies."

"Adele," the fireman called from where he'd moved closer to the dying flare to speak with a police officer. "You're going to want to hear this."

Adele puffed out her cheeks. "And yet I instantly doubt that I really do want to."

"Shall we?" Daniel's hand moved to the small of Adele's back.

As the group crossed the courtyard, lit by the flickering emergency service lights, the cop's gaze ranged over them. "Adele, this is completely off record until investigations confirm, but I'm giving you a heads-up so that you're alert."

"Sounds ominous, Steve." Adele shifted a tiny bit closer to Daniel. "What is it?"

"I worked closely with arson when I was in the city." A sea breeze tugged at the short sleeve of his uniform as Steve gestured toward the smoking rubble. "And I'm damn sure there was an incendiary device in the garbage can."

Adele crossed her arms over her chest. "You mean the rubbish caught fire? It couldn't." She swept one hand wide, indicating the paved sidewalk that linked the awning-fronted cafés and bars along the esplanade. "The strip's a no-smoking zone, so no smoldering butts." Her words picked up pace, jumbling together as though she'd prove him wrong. "And it's not like we serve flambé, heck, I don't even know how to flambé. Even the candles on the tables are battery operated. Down there"—she pointed—"Ocean's Sixty-Nine have tiki torches. But if they were going to cause a fire, it wouldn't be my business that burned down, would it?"

Steve pulled his phone from his pocket and checked the screen. "Investigations will be up from the city at first light. And I'm sorry, Adele, but I'm certain they're going to confirm my take. This wasn't an accident. There's material wadded in the bin, packed real tight. Doused in an accelerant to catch, it would've gone up with a bang. Then the palm leaves went up." He waved toward the building, as though any sign of the tropical hut look Adele had gone for, using giant palm fronds to disguise the cladding walls, was still evident. "Question is, Adele, not how but *who* would want to burn down The Little Blue?"

Hand encasing her fist, Adele pressed both her thumbs to her mouth, shaking her head. She seemed unaware of Daniel's hand steadying her. "No one. Jeez, Steve, you know I don't have enemies. Why would anyone do this? You're wrong. It has to be an accident." Her eyes watered.

Steve shook his head, his forehead furrowed. "Well, let's hope so. Or maybe it was kids or something. Just to be on the safe side, though, do you have somewhere you can spend the rest of the night? I don't want you going home alone."

Adele drew herself up straight. "I'm not

hammering on doors at this time of the morning, looking for charity." She seemed oblivious to the fact that the majority of the town was gathered in the street, watching the destruction of her livelihood.

Krissy patted at her boss's arm. "Stay at mine, Adele. We have a spare bed made up. Oh—" Her stomach clenched; only hours earlier, Erik hadn't wanted her to go home alone because—oh, God. Because she'd had a disagreement with a patron. A patron who Erik had been concerned might seek revenge.

Her gaze flew to him. "Could—?"

Brow furrowed, he gave her hand a reassuring squeeze. "No. I doubt it."

"What's that?" Steve whipped toward them. "You guys know something?"

Erik shook his head. "Not really. There was a bit of trouble here earlier, but I doubt it had anything to do with this."

"What sort of trouble?" Steve had his notebook out.

"Just drunks," Erik replied.

Krissy chewed on her lip for a second, but despite Erik's confidence, she wasn't so sure. "It was my fault. One of the customers was being handsy, and I overreacted—"

"Hang on, he laid hands on you?" Jax stiffened, his blue eyes blazing.

She shrugged. "No big deal. It happens. But tonight I'd had enough, and I whacked the dick instead of walking away."

"I hope you whacked his dick," Jax growled.

"I didn't want to make any contact with *that,*

thanks. Erik stepped in to save me and got into a brawl."

Erik snorted. "Hardly. It's not a bar fight—even an alfresco one—unless a chair gets broken. It was more a friendly caution." He thrust his hand into the pocket of his chinos, and she tried not to let her gaze linger on the bulge, hidden by night shadows. He turned to Steve. "There were three of them. Tourists. But they wouldn't have come back; they weren't the type to buy into more trouble than they could handle."

There was no doubt the lifeguard would bring more trouble than any normal guy could handle, but that didn't mean the jerks hadn't taken revenge on the sly. Guilt washed through Krissy. She'd been getting down and dirty with the lifeguards, while her prudish overreaction cost Adele her livelihood. "Adele, I'm so sorry. I should've ignored them and walked away."

Adele waved a dismissive hand. "We don't know it was them. And even if it was, that doesn't make it your fault. I've zero tolerance for any kind of harassment, whether it's of my staff or any other person. At least now the cops will have somewhere to start their search. Right, Steve?"

Steve tapped his pen against his notepad. "Right. Are you able to answer a few questions, Miss?"

Trent pointed across the courtyard to the café opposite. "You might not need too many questions. Isn't that a CCTV camera?"

Adele smacked her palm against her forehead. "Of course. Lord, I'm such an idiot. I'd completely forgotten—the Regional Tourism Board put cameras in a few years back, when we were having issues with out-of-hours drinking. Before your time, Steve." She screwed up her mouth. "Thing is, I don't know if they even work anymore."

Steve squinted up at the camera. "I'll get onto the Tourism Board as soon as they open. Find out where the data's uploaded. If there are cameras the full length of the strip, they may've picked up something useful." He turned back to Krissy. "Will you be pressing assault charges?"

She shook her head. "No. It was nothing. Really. Just typical touchy tourists, trying to get a bit extra for their money."

Jax's biceps bulged as his hands fisted. "Being on vacation doesn't make that shit okay."

That was the second time one of the lifeguards had reacted to the idea of another man touching her. Warning bells in her head matched the frantic pulse of the red and blue emergency service lights. "It was just a bar grope. Happens at least once a week."

"Not in my establishment, it doesn't." Adele shoved up the sleeves of her sweatshirt and picked across the ember-littered footpath toward her ruined building, accompanied by Trent, Tyson, and Daniel.

Steve tucked his notebook away. "I won't keep you now, but you'll need to make a formal statement at the station tomorrow."

"Can it be after work? I've only just started the job."

"I doubt The Little Blue will be reopening for business any time soon."

Yeah. Because of her. Because she'd been stupid enough to take offense at a lighthearted pass. She fiddled with the hem of her sarong. "The café's my part-time job. I work in—oh, shit." She slapped her palm across her eyes.

"What is it?" Erik's fingers fastened around her upper arms, forcing her to look up at him.

"Nothing. Like, really, nothing." Not on the scale of Adele's problems, anyway. "I just realized that I won't be getting Seagull vet checked anytime soon." In fact, along with still paying half the rent on the flat she'd shared with Brandon, she'd be pushing to feed the rescue. If the cat spread fleas and God-only-knew-what-else around their place, her sister would be unbearable.

She was already borderline insufferable.

"I know people. We'll work something out," Erik said.

The bells in her head rang louder. Working something out would require them seeing each other again. Which went against all her plans for a hot, fun, no-strings-attached fling. And she didn't want that.

Correction: she *shouldn't* want that.

"It's fine, I'll sort it." She angled her back to Erik and Jax. No fixating on one guy, and no one guy would have a claim on her.

Of course, Jax and Erik were two guys.

"Okay." Steve buttoned the flap of his pocket shut. "I'll be in touch tomorrow. Well, today, I guess."

She shivered as a breeze swirled around her legs. The dying crackle of the fire drew her gaze to where Adele surveyed the sludge of ash and charred leaves. The firefighter clumsily patted her boss's arm as Adele shook her head, hand covering her mouth. Daniel moved behind her, his broad shoulders protecting her from the ogling crowd.

As Krissy approached, Adele turned luminous eyes toward her, pinching at her quivering lips. It seemed the shock was only now setting in. "I'm sorry, Krissy, I'm going to have to let you go."

Her mouth opened uselessly. What could she say? It'd been her fault, and no amount of guilt or apology would bring Adele's café back. Or feed Seagull.

Adele knuckled her lips with a trembling hand. "Pete said the gas cylinders exploded and took out a wall. The kitchen's totaled. Guess I can't have much of a café without a kitchen." She managed a watery smile. "Though I could still serve drinks from the bar, as long as they don't require anything fancier than a slice of orange. But I'll have to let the casual staff go while I try to get back on my feet. I'm really sorry, hon."

Adele was apologizing to *her*? "God, don't worry about me. Look, crash at my place tonight, and when I get off work tomorrow, I'll come over and help you clean up what we can. Maybe it won't look quite so bad in the daylight."

Adele nodded. "I'd appreciate the help, if you have time. But no need for a room. I know you have a life." Her boss managed to quirk an eyebrow in Erik's direction.

"Nothing important." She stiffened her spine and folded her arms across her abdomen. The men were supposed to be nothing more than vibrators in human form.

Holy hell, that form, though.

But their micro-reactions and words made it clear they were already feeling some kind of ownership of her. It was time to find a different guy. Or a new vibrator. "I'll head home, then. See you tomorrow afternoon."

"Home-home?" Erik's hand fell from the small of

her back.

"Yeah. This was fun." She waved a vague hand. Hopefully, the others weren't counting just how many people she included in the gesture. Because. Well. Three. So close, she'd been so close to having both men.

She took a breath, forcing the words out. "Fun, but I have to be up early for work. The city's a fair drive. As you know," she added, remembering his cats.

Erik's jaw hardened. "Like I said, the choice is always yours. But we'll come up and check your house over, okay?"

She started to shake her head, but he continued. "As friends. Nothing more."

Dammit, she didn't want him—them—as a "nothing more." But she had no choice. Anything more was too dangerous.

Jax scowled. "You still reckon these guys are trouble, bro?"

"It doesn't hurt to be cautious."

"I'm fine," Krissy declared, though sudden nerves niggled at her. Malicious damage was one thing, but would the creeps take their anger further? "Besides, my housemate will be home by now. Don't worry about it."

Jax shook his head. "Sorry. This is the one area where you don't get any say. We'll check your house, then be out of your way, all right?"

Daniel interrupted. "Maybe we should keep watch overnight."

"Can't hurt," Erik agreed.

Daniel's glance cut to Adele. "You lads take Krissy's place, and I'll do Adele's."

Tyson smirked. "Don't you need company, Dad?

Take Trent."

"I'll be fine by myself. From what I gather, Trent wouldn't be much use to me, anyway."

Trent held up both hands, palms exposed. "Yup, Jayde's never going to be *that* understanding."

Krissy frowned, trying to make sense of the conversation, but Steve cleared his throat, slicing a hand through the air to cut the discussion off. "Sorry, gents, I know you're trying to help, but I can't condone any vigilante action. Tell you what, I'll patrol both houses every hour."

"Sure," Erik agreed too easily, and Krissy suspected he meant to set up camp on her doorstep regardless of the legal directive.

Good. She'd sleep better that way.

Or not sleep, knowing these two gorgeous men, men who *wanted* her, were meters away.

And now she couldn't have them at all.

Chapter Nine

If he'd driven alone, the cruise might've helped him get his head straight. Hell, even if he'd taken old Midge with him and been forced to listen to blues music, he could've done some thinking while he drove. Instead, he was subjected to Jax's monologue about where they'd go fishing that night.

Which was the perfect plan. Of course it was. Exactly what he wanted to do, right? They were headed into the city to scope out some details from the Fisheries Department, and he could comm the info back to Trent and Daniel. He was off duty, so there was nothing to stop them from hanging, checking out a couple of bars. No reason to rush home.

Except he wanted to get back.

To The Bay.

To The Point.

To Krissy.

Man, that was fucked. He was fucked.

For whatever reason, last night she'd said no. By the law of the Mer, he couldn't approach her again.

He slammed his palms on the steering wheel. Damn Jax for finding out her name. They were always easier to forget without a name. Always had been easy, anyway. What the hell was different about Kr—this one?

He cornered too fast, despite the warning from the

GPS. Was it her air of vulnerability, the impossible mix of outrageous desire and innocence?

There'd been plenty of girls who played innocent, intuitively knowing the best way to appeal to his jaded appetite, even if they didn't understand the reason for his cynicism; with centuries behind him and potentially millennia in front, there could never be any truly new experiences to sate his eternal hunger.

But that was the thing; the women had all been acting. Feigning demureness, protesting modesty, pretending surprise at his desires. All an act. To be keen to hook up with a couple of strangers, the woman had to have been around a bit, to have a modicum of experience under her garter belt.

Except for Krissy.

The car squealed into the gray shade of the underground parking lot.

"What's eating you, man?" Jax unclenched his fingers from the oh-shit handle above his window only after the vehicle came to a standstill.

He pulled the keys from the ignition. "Just stressing about the job. Senior Council will be all up our tails if we don't provide the details on the fleet ownership."

"Why would we have a problem? Pay our money, take our info. Government departments are slow, not impenetrable." Jax cracked his door open, the fumes of petrol and gas trapped in the cement tomb rushing in.

"We'll get the information. Thing is, I'm not keen on handing it over to Trent."

The loose coins in the console grated as Jax grabbed a handful. "Dying for coffee. I think I used up a year's supply of adrenaline last night, getting all fired up for nothing."

"You kidding? You knocked back an entire pot, already." For that matter, so had he, trying to clear the blurry eyes caused by keeping watch on Krissy's house until he was certain the tourists had checked in at the airport. Now the caffeine rush combined with lack of food and sexual frustration to put him on edge.

Jax shoved the change into the pocket of his shorts. "Why keep the ownership details from Trent?"

"Because I can't trust him with this." He winced. Words he'd never expected to utter. There again, he was experiencing feelings he'd never anticipated, either. Best he didn't think about that, though, and kept his focus on Trent's problems. "You didn't see him when they hurt Jayde. He was fit to kill them, and that was before he realized he wanted to bond with her. Now they have bonded..." He shook his head. "I'm worried he'll be out for revenge. And that's going to end badly for everyone concerned. At the very least, the Mer will be compromised. At worst, Trent could be in all kinds of shit." Dead, even. He hadn't healed from the bullet wound as quickly as he should. Maybe because he'd been dehydrated, the constant need for moisture the one chink in the Mer's scaly armor.

But maybe not because of that, at all.

Jax clambered out, stretching as though the confines of the large vehicle had cramped him, and spoke over the roof of the SUV. "If you guys are right about the rogue Mer turning traitor, we're already compromised. All we can do is hope to manage the leak, maybe twist it to some kind of PR advantage. Write the story off as an eco-publicity stunt. Elena will be all over that. But for her to get her seagulls in a row, we need to get the facts to the Council. Don't worry, Dad will keep Trent in line."

"Hope so." He beeped the car and strode across the deserted parking lot toward the stairwell.

Jax matched his pace. "Until the Council can come up with some info on what happens with a part-Mer bond, Trent needs to play it safe. What if Jayde being part Mer isn't enough to preserve his immortality? What if he has, like, only so many lives now? Y'know, a catfish with nine lives." He grinned, but his eyes didn't share the joke.

"Yeah. That's what's eating me, bro. How do you test immortality? Seems like it's a yes-no deal, with no safe in-between."

He bolted the six flights of stairs, as though the expenditure of energy could purge his thoughts. Light streamed through the doorway on level three, and he blinked, acclimating his eyes to the electric glare.

As he stepped into the room, he hunched his shoulder to block the sight of an aquarium bubbling in the corner. Closed his mind so he wouldn't hear the faint pleas emitting from the glass prison. He couldn't rescue every damn clownfish in every office block in every city. Funny how humans touted the therapeutic qualities of aquarium keeping. Not so beneficial for their captives.

It'd taken them a couple of hours to reach the city, and the office already had several clients, perched on uncomfortable-looking seats around the edges of the room, waiting for God-only-knew-what. That was another thing about humans. They were reactive, rather than proactive. He strode across the unpopulated center of the room toward the reception counter, a scarred wooden bench exposed by unforgiving strip lighting.

The receptionist had her back to him, so he smacked the silver bell on the counter. As she turned, she shoved the swoop of blonde hair from her face.

His heart lurched to a standstill. Krissy.

"Huh." Alongside him, Jax's breath escaped in a rush. *Awesome! Lunch break hookup?*

He shook his head. Krissy had blown them off last night. They needed to be sure of her interest before pursuing her. Clear consent. "I didn't realize you worked here."

Krissy frowned, a line furrowing between her chestnut eyes. She glanced around the room and lifted one shoulder. "No reason why you should. Is there?"

"Well, no. I guess not." Not the warmest reception he'd ever had.

"What can I do for you?"

His gaze flew to her face, searching for the twinkle of laughter that would acknowledge her double entendre. Nothing. "I, uh, I was wondering if you'd help me with an unusual request." He wasn't breaking Mer law, merely bending it a little. His words could be construed as innocent enough, if she chose not to take the bait.

Apparently, she wasn't hungry. "Which is?" Her fingers tapped at the keyboard hidden just below the ledge, though he'd given her no reason to input anything. Unless maybe she was searching "how to get rid of unwanted lovers." She wouldn't have to Google too long; her icy demeanor had a swifter effect on his semi-hard dick—which muscle memory had barred up the second he saw her—than a cold shower.

Ouch, dude. Wipeout. Jax shifted alongside him,

turning to check the room. No doubt looking for other candidates. He should do the same.

Except he didn't want to.

What he did want was to know what had changed Krissy's mind. She'd been totally into them before the fire. Was it because she blamed him for the incident? Did she think that, because he'd warned off the troublemakers, they'd come back…and that somehow reflected badly on her? Hells, she'd mentioned being short on cash because of the loss of her second job; was that the problem? He intended to make good on his offer of fixing up the cat's vet bill.

Taking his cue from her manner, he handed over the printed list of names. "I need to trace the registered owners of these vessels. I believe I can purchase a search?"

She glanced at the documents, the aggressive set of her shoulders relaxing a little. Okay, so she wanted to keep this transaction businesslike. Maybe because two other clerks sat a few feet away from her? She had mentioned this was a new job. "You can purchase a number of things across the counter."

Surely that had to be a come-on?

If it was, her poker face was admirable. She focused on her monitor. "Give me a few minutes. I'll complete the search now. The price schedule is above your head." She jerked a finger up at the list taped to the glass screen.

Only hours earlier, those fingers had been wrapped around his cock. Days earlier, chasing his cum from her chin.

Dammit, what was wrong with him?

Jax snorted. *Wow. Frostier than a sea-witch's tit.*

Move on, man.

Yeah. His cousin was right. Yet still, he delayed.

Krissy flicked her gaze up, eyes hard as creek pebbles. "Was there something else?"

He shook his head. "It seems not."

She pointed toward the row of seats against the wall. "Take a seat. I'll have to charge you for four separate searches, though it seems the vessels are owned by the same parent entity. The department accepts payment by cash and all major cards. No personal checks, please."

Clearly, no personal *anything*.

He'd barely sat before she called him back, not by name, but by catching his gaze and jerking her head in a peremptory manner.

"Here's your information. Card or cash?"

As she took his card, swiping it through the reader, Jax leaned across the counter. She recoiled, lifting an eyebrow.

Unfazed by her glacial demeanor, Jax drummed his fingers on the wood. "Hey, Krissy, did you hear anything new on The Little Blue this morning?"

Krissy's fingers stilled on the keypad. "Why would I?"

Jax shoved a strand of hair behind his ear. "Just thought Adele or that cop—what was his name, Steve?—might've called about the CCTV footage."

Krissy's hand flew to her mouth, almost fast enough to hide the tiny smile that played at the corner of her lips. "Oh. I see. No, can't say I heard from either of them. Thank you." She turned away, making a business of stacking her papers together.

Jax rolled his eyes and shrugged. *Moving right*

along...go with the flow, bro.

Why the hell couldn't he drum up the same indifference? Wasn't like it was the first time he'd ever struck out.

Only the first time he'd cared.

****

It was coincidence he headed to the beach at the same time as he'd met Krissy there the other day. Off duty, he didn't need to bring in the flags or lock up the station. He just happened to like this particular stretch of beach.

And maybe Krissy did, too.

Nothing in the Mer rules about him swimming in the same spot she did.

She wasn't there, though. He stripped off his shirt and dropped it with his phone. In approximately the same place Krissy had laid her towel earlier in the week.

Okay, in exactly the same place.

Again, coincidence.

He waded into the ocean and dove through the light surf, striking out to the nets that sectioned the bay. He'd check them for any trapped marine life. They were a necessary evil, keeping the swimmers safe from predators, but that was no reason for the Mer to let ocean life perish in them. All of The School checked the nets multiple times a day, though they could simply attune their minds to the distress calls.

He worked along the net methodically, weaving back broken strands where a shark had ripped free. Hopefully, the fish had learned his lesson and taken off for the deeper ocean. Which is what he should be doing, instead of hanging around the shallows like a seagull scavenging scraps.

Scraps of Krissy's attention.

She'd dismissed him today, but why? And what had been the reason behind her smile, that tiny glimmer of promise, as he left? He'd made an idiot of himself, hanging back a fraction of a second too long, praying she'd cast a crumb of hope in his direction. Busy with her paperwork, she'd not even glanced his way, her face hidden by the gorgeous swoop of hair, the demure black skirt cupping her taut backside as she moved between the desks, dropping files and picking up other papers. What the hells had happened to the lustful, intriguing, wanton woman of last night?

When he realized the other two office employees were staring at him, he'd followed Jax. They'd headed to a couple of bars, where he'd doused his misery in coffee rather than beer. Years of experience meant he knew alcohol would make him maudlin.

But his misery had never been focused on a woman before.

Jax had also lamented Krissy's loss, but in a far more pragmatic fashion. Plenty more fish in the ocean, he'd said. Quite correctly. He'd used the line himself, trying to persuade Trent not to fixate on Jayde.

Of course, Trent had fixated. And Trent was happy now. But against all odds, and yet to be accepted by Senior Council, Trent had found a part-Mer woman.

He already knew Krissy most definitely was not Mer.

Yet that didn't make him want her any less.

Damn.

He carved through the ocean, his mind churning like the waves, trying not to think. The sun had sunk by the time he realized Jax was mind-tapping him.

Bro, where'd you get to? Adele contacted Dad.

Daniel? Odd. Adele had both his number and Trent's.

Yeah. Don't ask. I reckon I may be getting an extra birthday card this year. New mama. Courtesy of Gramps, the Mer had a relaxed attitude to polyamorous relationships, even among their own kind. *Anyway, your police mate got hold of the CCTV footage. He's been trying to contact you. Needs you to go see if you can ID anyone.*

His feet hit the sand, and he strode from the shallows, crossing the darkened beach. *Okay. I'll head over now.*

He refused to ask whether Krissy had already viewed the footage.

She was in the tiny police station, a mere two offices, manned for only a couple of hours a day, standing alongside Adele. Now was the perfect opportunity to discover whether her freeze earlier had been due to her work environment. He blew out a tense breath. Raked his hands through his hair.

The reception desk unattended, the two women pored over paperwork on the high laminate counter.

He strode up behind them. "Are these the pictures we're to look at?"

Adele glanced up and smiled. "Hey, Erik. Yeah, Steve had these stills printed from the footage."

Krissy turned toward him, but her face remained expressionless. Shit. Not a good sign.

He flicked a hand toward the prints. "Do they look like those jerks to you?"

Krissy shrugged. "How would I know?"

Again, he caught the ghost of a smile, as though she teased him. But Gods knew, this wasn't a nice kind of teasing. He was close enough to smell her, though her perfume was different today. Sharper. He ran a hand around the inside of his collar, careful not to brush against her as he leaned forward.

Though maybe if he touched her…?

No. He wasn't welcome. That much was clear, even if the reason wasn't. Anger firmed his jaw even as disappointment weighted his chest. "Well, let me see, then."

"I'll let Steve know you're here," Adele said, heading toward the door into the inner office. "He's got the actual footage. I'm not sure the stills make the pictures any clearer."

He shoved a hand in his pocket. Asking Krissy's reason wouldn't break any Mer law. It wasn't like he was trying to coerce her. Of course, it *was* like he was being utterly pathetic. "Listen, Krissy, I'm not sure what I've done wrong—"

Krissy rasped one finger down the side of his face. "It's not so much that you've done anything wrong." She took her hand away, staring at her fingertips as though the feel of his stubble had been unfamiliar. "More that you're wrong for me."

"Okay. That's kind of conclusive." He forced the words through tight lips.

Krissy lifted one shoulder. "I'm sorry. But we're never going to get it on."

"I thought we pretty well had got it on." Maybe not to the ultimate finale, but surely what they *had* done counted? Sure as hell did in his books.

Something flared in her eyes. "And did you think I

enjoyed it?"

"Well, yeah. I thought you were fully into it, until we got interrupted."

"Was I?" she mused, one finger tapping her chin, her gaze moving to the ceiling as though she tried to recall a distant memory. "See, I find that hard to believe, because you're so not my type. I don't mean to be rude, you're cute and all, but"—she waved a hand up and down his front—"by yourself, you're not bringing anything I'm interested in buying."

"I know. That's why Jax came over, remember?"

"Jax?" Lines of puzzlement creased Krissy's forehead.

What had he walked into? His distant cousin, Lethe, had a penchant for wiping mortal memories, but he'd not seen evidence of her tricks for decades. "Yeah. Jax. You know, last night. Remember you wanted us to—"

"Whoa!" She thrust a hand up to stop his words. A smile flashed across her face, erasing the stern facade. "TMI. But no, I don't know. And I'm pretty sure I don't *want* to know what my big—"

"Erik!"

The door to the office banged open, and he whirled toward the sound of his name. On Krissy's lips. Then he turned one-hundred-and-eighty degrees back to face…Krissy.

"What—?"

Krissy number two fisted her hands on her hips, glaring at Krissy number one. "Really, Christie. Again?"

"Wait…Christie?" He squinted at the woman closest to him, noticing for the first time the almost imperceptible scar on her sardonically tilted upper lip. Not the lips he'd so intently watched fasten around his cock. But the lips of the woman from the Fisheries Office.

Accompanied by the sergeant, Adele stepped from the inner office, her glance raking the three of them. She guffawed, a deep belly laugh. "Krissy didn't mention she's a twin, Erik? I guess the girls are still new around here, but it's not like you to miss this kind of an opportunity. Let me introduce you to both Krystal and Christina."

Krissy, no, *Christie*, held up her hand. "No opportunity here, Adele. I was just telling Erik my interests are not the same as Krissy's."

Krissy dashed across the office, her hip brushing his like the kiss of an electric eel. She crossed her arms over her chest, directing a scowl at her sister. "Seriously, Christie, isn't this trick a bit past its use-by? How old are you, anyway?"

"Old enough to know better, young enough not to care." Christie tossed her hair back. "Unlike you, big sis. Making out like you're a nun after dumping Mr. Beige, yet hooking up with…" Her eyebrows nearly hit her hairline as she looked him up and down. "And who the heck is Jax?"

"Jax?" Adele's interest flared.

Erik winced. They tried to keep their fishing techniques on the down-low as far as the locals were concerned. "You know, Daniel's son," he said, hoping to distract the café owner.

"Oh. Yes. Dan." Adele's words were breathy. Instant success.

Krissy's fingertips wandered across the back of his

hand, weaving a trail of relief through him. Relief he shouldn't feel, because there should be no emotion attached to this fling. Zero. None. Zip.

She slanted a look up at him, a mix of sadness and maybe a little fear. "Those creeps weren't on the footage."

"The angles aren't great, so we don't have the actual incident," Steve said. "You mind taking a look, Erik, see if you can identify anyone?"

"Sure." He threaded his fingers through Krissy's. He was still trying to process what had happened, deal with the tidal-rip surges of hope and disappointment, but in the interim, she wasn't getting away again.

"In here." Steve shoved the door. "It'll only take a minute, as there wasn't much traffic after close of business. Not unless you count the feral cats."

"That reminds me, Krissy," Erik said. "I booked Seagull in for a vet check next Friday, if that's cool with you?"

She pulled back. "No, not yet. I can't afford it for a while."

"I have a frequent-customer freebie kind of thing. The voucher expires soon, and I've no use for it." Not giving her a chance to voice her disbelief, he planted his hands on the desk in the tiny office and leaned over the computer. "Okay, hit me, Sarge." He'd give this a quick once-over, and then he could talk to Krissy, work out what had— His breath stuck on an inhale, and his shoulders locked. He clenched his teeth to subdue the urge to comm what he was seeing to Trent. "Can you run it again, Steve?"

The tape flickered, then replayed.

He kept his tone controlled, despite the adrenaline

pumping through his veins. "Nobody I know, but how about I get Trent to come in and take a look? He mentioned seeing a few memorable characters around the place recently."

Chapter Ten

She'd spent the night lying awake, thinking about the lifeguards. And heck, yeah, if she was honest, she'd spent the day thinking about them, too. Two gorgeous men servicing her, what the hell else was she supposed to think about? Even quitting work early to help Adele salvage what she could from the café hadn't provided much of a distraction, as she'd been constantly on the lookout for the lifeguards.

After chasing them off. Damn. Had she been too quick to make up her mind, shut them down too hard and fast? Maybe Adele's café wasn't the only thing around here that'd been burned.

Daniel had come by in the late afternoon, accompanied by the most stunning woman she'd ever seen. Adele had chatted animatedly over coffee with the pair, the pheromones from her flirtation with Daniel thicker than the smell of char.

When they left, she donned her gloves, picked up a sponge, and returned to help Krissy scrub at a blackened section of the wall. She blew a wisp of hair from her face. "I can't tell you how much I appreciate your help, hon. But you've done enough, you worked right through the coffee break. You should've joined us. Dan's so interesting to talk with."

Krissy shook the cramp out of her arm. "Uh huh. Interesting? That's the descriptor you want to go with?"

Adele giggled. "Okay, the man is sex on legs. Is that what you want to hear?"

"It's more where my own mind was going. What's the deal with Elena, though? She's with him?"

Adele sloshed water on the wall. "No idea. She's gorgeous, isn't she? Yet she gives off the saddest vibe I've ever picked up on. Like, not a depressed aura, but a genuinely sad feeling, as though there's tragedy in her history." Adele's hand closed around the rainbow of polished crystal chips strung around her neck, fingering them as if she counted rosary. "Actually, I should check if I have a nice piece of citrine. Or maybe a smoky quartz. If Elena had an improved energy field, that might help. Mind, with Daniel around, I'd have thought the energy couldn't get much better." She waggled her eyebrows.

Krissy dunked her sponge in the mucky water. "It doesn't bother you she's with Daniel? Or sort of with Daniel?"

Adele almost dropped her rag. "You mean am I jealous? No, hon, of course not. Why on Earth would I be?"

"Well, you do *like* Daniel, right?"

"Like him? One look at that man and my ovaries…" She pantomimed an explosion in front of her soft stomach.

"So exploding lady parts, but no jealousy?"

Applying the rag vigorously to the wall, Adele shook her head. "No room in life for those kinds of emotions, hon. If you bring negative energy, it'll just double back on you. I like the man. He either likes me, or he doesn't. Neither will change my life, and you can be darn sure I won't change my life to make it happen, either. We gotta live in the moment, Krissy. What will be, will be."

"Oh, my God." The sponge fell from her nerveless fingers.

"What is it? Sit down. You look like you're taking a bad trip."

The breath wheezed out of her as she shook her head. "No. No, I'm fine. I just realized where I've been going wrong." She'd sent Jax and Erik away last night, not because she didn't trust them, but because she didn't trust herself to enjoy hot sex without emotional entanglement. She'd been terrified she'd confuse lust with love. Yet the truth was, it didn't matter which emotion she felt, as long as she allowed herself to feel. She was hungry for passion, for excitement, for adventure…and it was self-denial that made her miserable. Not Brandon. He didn't have that kind of power over her. No one did.

She'd thought that by allowing herself to be wild and free, to have sex with anyone, any way she wanted, she'd be liberated. But there could be no freedom if she kept her heart caged. It wasn't only in her sex games she needed to abolish the rules; her emotions needed emancipating, too.

Live in the moment.

"Wow." She was grinning like an idiot, but the epiphany freed her.

****

The second she saw Erik in the police station, desire settled thick and syrupy in her pelvis. She knew precisely what she needed to do.

She could screw Erik and Jax and then spend hours analyzing and agonizing over how she felt about sex and commitment and connection and feelings.

Or she could screw Erik and Jax and enjoy the experience, accept however she felt—because analysis was merely a route to guilt.

As Erik suggested Trent come in to view the tape, Steve shook his head. "No, I'm headed out on patrol now. Would he be available tomorrow morning?"

"Sure." Erik nodded. "He's not rostered on at the station. About nine? I'll have to drag him off the love nest."

"Adele mentioned he's hooked up—one of the biologists from the research center, right?" Steve flipped off the monitor. "Can we make it eight? I'm not on duty, but I'll swing by then."

"Done." As Steve ushered them from the room, Erik dropped his arm to her waist. "There's a beautiful full moon tonight. It'll be best viewed from the beach."

She grimaced, brushing both hands down her front, slowing on her breasts. "Sandy." His face fell, and she grinned. "Ocean?"

"Sure." Erik's lips brushed her ear as they entered the outer office. "Just so you're aware, I'm never going to say no to watching you get wet."

Either his words or his low, sexy drawl contained some kind of magic, because the second he said it, she was. She licked her lips, hoping her voice wouldn't come out pitchy. "Adele, I'm going for a swim to clean off a bit of the grime."

"Or to get dirty?" Christie smirked. That was the problem with having a twin, too much mind-reading going on.

"Sure, hon." Adele flapped a hand at her. "You've done more than enough, so call it quits. Wouldn't catch me swimming once the sun goes down, though."

"I'm sure I'll be safe." She would. Her heart, her emotions, and her body. Because she was fully in control now.

"You know I'll make sure you are." Erik ducked his chin. "Adele. Christie—I'd say nice to meet you, but I'm not quite convinced yet."

Her sister grinned unrepentantly. "Of course it was nice. I'm the improved version of Krissy."

Erik's arm tightened around her. "She doesn't need any improvement."

As they strolled through the twilight toward the beach, her cell vibrated in the bag slung across her shoulder. She'd forgotten it was switched to silent, and there were a number of messages to flick through. As she read each, her smile grew, the excitement bubbling within her.

"Good news?" Erik sounded amused.

"Awesome news." Her thumb hovered over the phone for a moment as she debated telling him. She didn't want to sound like she was bragging, but this was kind of huge. "I know you never thought the arsonist was that idiot from last night, and according to the footage, you're right." She paused, giving him the opportunity to crow.

Instead, he looked pensive, frowning into the distance as though the thought of the footage triggered more in him than a desire to I-told-you-so her. So not Brandon.

"Okay. Anyway, I felt guilty about the whole business, regardless. And I was thinking about it in bed last night. For some reason, I had trouble sleeping."

He smirked. "I'd rather you'd been thinking about

other things, but I guess that's understandable."

His insinuation of their sexual history made her heart beat so loud she could barely hear the surf crashing against the rocky outcrop at the far curve of the beach. She dragged in a ragged breath and hurried on. "I figured The Little Blue is probably Adele's sole income."

"I imagine so. She's been there for over a decade."

"That's what the other retailers along the strip told me." She kicked off her flipflops and bent to pick them up. Erik's hand glided down her back to the curve of her butt, as though touching her up in public was the most natural thing in the world. Her toes curled in the warm sand as her lips curved.

"The other retailers?" His hands spanned her waist as she straightened.

"Yeah. Anyway, only her kitchen is damaged, so technically, the café and bar could still function, if Adele had food to serve."

"Your logic seems impeccable." Erik maneuvered her so her back was against the smooth bark of a frangipani tree, a whisper of heavily perfumed air separating their bodies. "Except that a café without food seems somewhat redundant. A little like sex without kissing." Green gaze pinioning her, he lowered his head, the warmth of his lips tantalizingly brushing past her cheeks, her chin.

She whimpered, arching toward him, desperate for what he promised but denied.

Finally, he reached her lips.

A sweet kiss, long and lingering, one of his hands stroking her hair, the other chastely on her waist, yet it fired her blood as much as any of his sensual caresses.

Why had she ever thought she needed to ban this pleasure in order to retain her sense of self?

When they finally broke apart, Erik reached to pluck a waxy bloom from a branch above them and tucked it behind her ear. Then he traced his fingers down her cheek, a smile curving his lips. "You were saying?"

"Yes. I was…something." The thoughts flitted around in her head, ricocheting with the excitement of his nearness. "It doesn't matter. I'll tell you later. Is Jax at your place tonight?"

"Do you want him to be?"

Yes. But maybe that was now because she wanted him, not because she needed him. A flash of pride tweaked the corner of her lips up. Nothing like a little emotional growth to make her feel like a woman. Well, nothing, except for the caresses of this sexy man. "I do. But maybe a little later?"

He paused a beat, his gaze faraway, then smiled down at her. "Done. How about I take you out for dinner first?"

Dinner inferred a date, not a hookup. Acceptance would flout the boundaries she'd set herself.

Ridiculously strict, unnecessary boundaries, which no longer had reason to exist. *What will be, will be.* She slid her hands beneath his shirt, relishing the brush of her fingers against his ridged flesh. "I planned to grab some takeaway and make sure Adele eats. She's barely stopped working all day."

Erik turned so his gaze ranged the white-capped ocean. "Daniel's heading in—over, I mean—with the same plan."

"Again? He was here earlier today with…Elena, is

it?"

"Seems he's sweet on her."

"On Elena?"

Erik shook his head. "Elena's like a daughter to him."

"So you think Daniel likes Adele? Your uncle does have a certain charm." She ducked beneath Erik's arm, tiny spumes of sand fountaining in front of her feet as she raced across the beach.

"Does he now?" Erik's eyes glittered as he effortlessly matched her pace.

"A family trait maybe?" She untied her sarong and let it drop at the edge of the water.

Erik tugged his shirt over his head, and her breath hitched as the moon silver-etched the muscles and planes of his body. His hands encircled her waist, pulling her hips against him, his heat warding off the slight nighttime chill. "You're a fine one to question about family. You've no idea what went through my head when I met your sister this morning."

"This morning? You only met Christie just now." She pointed toward the fairy lights of the town.

Erik nuzzled her neck. Sparks flew through her as every nerve end responded to his touch. Her skin tingled, her core aching for his touch.

"No," Erik said. "At her office in the city. She gave me and Jax the cold shoulder, and I figured we—" He planted a kiss on her lips. "—were through."

"Through?" She arched an eyebrow. "Oh, no, I have plans." She grabbed the hem of her shirt and tugged it off.

Lust flared his pupils. "I like the sound of that. And the look of that."

His hand moved to cup her breast, but she stopped him. "I want what you keep promising me." She dropped her panties and spun, striding through the shallows to dive into the exhilarating terror of the dark ocean.

Blue-black crystals sparkled in Erik's hair as he surfaced beside her without a splash, fluorescence clinging to his skin. "But—"

"No." She held up her hand. "I heard you. I heard your cautions and your restrictions. But I don't care."

The water sheeted from him as he stood, pulling her close. Her nipples pebbled against his muscled torso as his hands cupped her butt, the water lapping below the crease of her cheeks. *God.* A great, fluttering cloud of butterflies erupted in her stomach; Erik must've stripped his shorts back on the shore. A rigid bar, his erection pressed into her lower belly.

She knew how that cock looked.

How it tasted.

How it fit in her hand, satin-covered steel.

But she wanted more.

She skimmed her hands up his chest, then gripped the back of his neck. "I need to know how you feel inside me. No more teasing. I want you to fuck me." She pressed her bottom into his kneading hands. "Fuck me *there*."

"There? You mean you want me to fuck you in the ass?" He moved his mouth to her ear, his words rough and low with desire. "You know my rules, Krissy. You have to say it." His hands separated her cheeks, delving into her pussy for lubrication, then slicking up the crease of her butt. He found her tight hole, his finger pressing against the intimate pucker of flesh. "Here,

Krissy? You want my fat cock in here?"

"Yes." She could barely get the word out around the excitement and lust raging within her. "Yes, I want you to fuck me there. Now."

"Oh, fuck, I want that, too." He spun her around to face the ocean and locked one arm around her waist, his erection nudging her butt. Hips grinding against her, he thrust shallowly along her slit, each surge tickling her clit as she writhed against him, trying to guide him to the position she wanted.

"You have to get my cock good and wet, Krissy," he breathed in her ear. "Are you wet for me?"

"Uh huh." Her reply came out on a sob of desire as he teased her.

Knuckles grazing her bottom, he gripped his cock in a chokehold and stroked it up and down her ass, easing her cheeks apart.

Each pass deeper.

Slower.

Tantalizingly closer to where she wanted—needed—him to be.

"Like this, Krissy? Is this what you want?"

"Yes," she moaned as the domed helmet pressed against the sensitive pout of her core. Yes, she needed him there so badly.

"More?"

"Yes. Oh!" she gasped, her taut muscle unfurling like a flower as he eased the pulsing head of his cock into her. "Oh, my God!"

"Too much?" Tension trembled through the arm he had locked around her waist as Erik restrained himself, the tip of his cock stretching her open.

She blew out between pursed lips, the pleasure and

pain an exquisite blend. "More." She rocked back against him, her thighs quivering as she tried to force him farther inside.

"Ah, baby," he groaned. "My Gods, you're awesome. So fucking tight." His tongue found her ear as his free hand slid over her stomach, trailing phosphorescence down to her slit, spreading her juice to lubricate both of them. She shifted her feet wider, and he hooked two fingers inside her, the heel of his hand expertly applying pressure to the hard nub of her clit.

Her knees buckled, and she closed her eyes. Grit her teeth, trying to push farther back, to take more of him. "Fuck me," she implored.

"Not yet," he cautioned. "No more until you're really ready. When you want to come, you tell me."

"Then what?" she panted, her hips undulating with the movement of his fingers.

"Then," he murmured, "when you want to come so bad that you're screaming to have me inside you, I'm going to fuck your sweet ass. You said you need me to come, to prove how much I really want you? Well, I'm going to pound my cock into you, and while you're coming, your tight little body is going to milk me. I'm going to fuck a load of cum right up your ass, Krissy."

"Oh, fuck," she moaned. So dirty, so perfect, his words tipped her over the edge. She bent forward, the tips of her hair sweeping the water as she thrust back against him. "Oh fuck, do it now. Do it now, Erik, I'm coming. Fuck me, fuck me now!"

He surged inside her, heat and power and desire, filling her so completely as the stars showered the ocean and she shuddered and writhed, impaled on his cock, the orgasm stealing her feet, spiraling her brain, spinning the world until she could no longer tell sea from sky.

As she quivered and shook, Erik's arm around her waist held her safe. His fingers worked her clit, letting her come down, the tremors slowing as she recaptured her sobbing breath. Then he slowly withdrew. "All right?"

"More than all right." She felt exultant. Accomplished. A woman. Alive in ways she'd never believed possible. She'd done what she'd longed to do, lived her fantasy, and she'd damn well enjoyed it.

Hell, no, she'd loved it.

Erik wrapped both arms around her waist from behind, tugging her so her head lay back against his shoulder and he could kiss the curve of her jaw. "And now I can buy you dinner?"

"Unless you want a repeat?"

"Oh, you'd better believe that I do. But I also need to refuel." He took her hand as they waded from the shallows. "So are you willing to rethink your dislike of sex on the beach?"

She grinned. "I'll concede you've expanded my horizons. Next you'll have me believing in unicorns and mermaids."

"Indeed." He paused a beat, looking at her consideringly, then his lips twisted in a tight smile that seemed almost melancholy. "And are you still interested in expanding other horizons?"

Oh, hell, yes, she was interested in anything he had to offer. "Do you have suggestions?"

Erik pulled her to a halt. He cupped her face between his hands, shook his head a fraction. "I can think of so many things I want to try with you. Starting with…have you ever been kissed to an orgasm?"

He'd blown her no-kissing rule right out of the water, so she may as well go all in. She'd never be able to get enough of his lips on hers, the way he made her feel as though kissing would be enough, an erotic act all by itself. "Is that even possible?"

The flash of his cocky, sexy smile said he believed it entirely so. "I move we find out. But first, we eat."

They dressed and then crossed the foreshore, finding Daniel in the café with Adele, drinking port in the front bar, which showed little evidence of the fire.

Adele looked over the rim of her glass. "Oh, Krissy, hon, I meant to give you the collection box to take in to work with you this morning. I know they're not expecting it until the end of the month, but it's not like we'll be picking up any more donations for a while. And it's not safe here until the wall's repaired."

"I'll get it now." She crossed to the counter and retrieved the Perspex box, tucking it under her arm, but Erik took it from her. He turned it in his large hands, reading the label. "Ocean Conservation Foundation? That's where you work?"

"Yeah, for the last eight years. Well, a month here, but I was in the head office before that."

Amusement curved his lips. "You don't like sand or…"

She caught a glint of laughter in Daniel's eyes, as though he somehow knew what Erik held back from saying.

"…or *stuff* on the beach, but you work for Ocean Conservation?"

She took the box from him, tossing her wet hair primly over one shoulder. "I'm all about what goes on *in* the water, not on the beach."

"Oh, don't I know that," he murmured, seeming oblivious to Adele's interest.

Well, she could be, too. She pressed in closer to him. "But I'm open to persuasion…"

Desire surged in Erik's eyes, his nostrils flaring. Forget about food; she wanted more of him.

Daniel cleared his throat. "Jax said to let you know he'll be at your place by the time you get there, Erik."

Adele would have whiplash in the morning, her neck practically cracking as she looked from Daniel, to them, and back again, but it was Erik's frown that confused Krissy. He knew the deal. Two guys, no complications. It had been his suggestion.

She met Adele's huge-eyed gaze. "Live in the moment, right?" She swiveled back to Erik. "We should skip dinner if Jax is waiting." A flush crawled up her cheeks, but she refused to let it rule. "I need a word with Daniel first, though. Alone."

Chapter Eleven

What on Earth did Krissy have to speak with Daniel about?

Curious as he was, he refused the urge to tap his uncle's mind as he and Krissy stood on the far side of the room, heads close together.

Didn't stop him from staring as though he could lip read, though. Not that he was jealous of his uncle—or anyone else. Thing was, he honestly had no issue with sharing women; hells, he'd done so since conception.

But there was no law against him wanting Krissy to like him *best*.

She glanced across the room, caught his perusal, and shot him a smile as she headed his way.

His heart slammed to a stop, then kicked back into gear.

"Are you okay?" She nodded at the hand rubbing his chest.

He glanced down at it. "Yeah. Sure. Must've pulled a muscle." What, while he was out swimming? Like that would ever happen. More like when he'd wrapped his arm around Krissy's slim waist, holding her as she bucked and writhed against him.

Hells, he shouldn't think about that. Not while they were in company, anyway. He moved behind a high-backed chair. "Are you ready to go?"

"Ready and wetting," she murmured.

He blew out a sharp breath. "Right. Car's down the road a bit. Near the cop shop."

"Race you." Her lips curved wickedly.

****

She wasn't the only one who could drive like a maniac when the need was pressing. And need wasn't the only thing pressing. He shifted in the leather car seat, trying to make room in his pants for his hard on. He'd briefly considered taking her down to the beach again—hell, *taking* her any way, anywhere he could—because it was closer. But if she'd ever let him, he still had firsts to check off, and for at least one of those, he needed Jax.

Plus, Krissy had made it clear she was keen to see Jax again.

Her hand edged up his thigh as he drove, and he covered it with his own. She curled her fingers around his, and he could feel her tension. "What's wrong, sweetheart?"

She shook her head, chewing on her lip. Turned to look out of the window, though he suspected it was more so she didn't have to face him than because she wanted to watch the palms flash past. "I was thinking. About the rules."

Gods, don't let her take kissing away! He'd been serious about the kissing-her-to-orgasm plan. "Thinking what, exactly?"

"Maybe we can renegotiate. Kind of mostly on the…no P in the V bit."

He chuckled. She'd let him touch her in the most intimate ways possible, flirted outrageously, gave the best deep throat he'd ever had, yet still she'd suddenly turn shy. He loved the mercurial changes in her mood, like sun splashing into the depths of the ocean. "So how do you envisage this restructure working? No issue with the whole Sunday paper thing now?"

She shook her head like she was brushing a thought aside. "Like you said, with Jax there, that won't happen. It's a different dynamic. Right?"

Yeah, the dynamic that kept him alive. "Right. Krissy, are you on birth control?" Manufacturers could say what they liked, and latex was a vast improvement on Goodyear's rubber units from a couple of hundred years ago, but with a condom on he wouldn't be able to *feel* her. He wanted to experience the suction of her velvet walls, aware of the tight ring of her cervix as he plunged deep within her, feel every tiny tremble and quiver of her warm tunnel as he...had sex with her. Yeah, that was all. Sex.

She tapped her lips. "Pill. And I've only had one partner. Until you," she added, managing to bring her gaze to the road in front of them.

He gripped the wheel tighter. Gods, when he'd thought she was unicorn-close to being a virgin, he'd not realized how correct his assessment was. One partner. And that guy had been a jackass who wasn't into her. Literally.

"So I'm clean. I mean—"

He could feel the heat radiating from her cheeks. "Krissy, my phone's in the dash there. Pull it out." He waited as she fumbled with it. "Go into the Health App and open the correspondence directory."

"Done."

"Click on the file labeled clinic."

She nodded as she read, her shoulders relaxing.

"Clean bill of health, dated last month." The Mer

always had a clean bill of health; immune to STDs, they neither carried nor suffered. But it was easier to have a test to prove it than explain the fantasy that was their reality. "Jax will have his results on him, too." He commed ahead, warning his cousin to offer to show Krissy his test. There was no reason for her to be embarrassed about something as smart as protecting herself.

The automatic roller door shut behind them as he pulled the SUV into his garage, but he made no move to get out. "So we're all good?"

She faced him now, the last of her reservations disappearing. "We are *so* good."

He probably looked like an idiot, he was grinning so wide. "Let's go in. Jax's got some grub on."

She swung her legs from the car but paused, looking back over her shoulder at him. "How can you know that? I only suggested not eating out like, ten minutes ago."

"Hunch." He'd have to be more careful.

The industrial stainless-steel kitchen aromatic with the rich scent of fried onion, Jax waved a spatula at them. "Home is the sailor…"

"R.L. would be proud of you."

"Stine?" Krissy said.

He folded his arms around her waist, so he could make eye contact with Jax above her head. "Stevenson. Jax is trying to woo you, quoting poetry."

"Only because my cooking is a little rusty. Hope pasta's good all round, it's about all I know how to make." Jax rattled pans on the cooktop.

"No tapas? All those years in Barcelona totally wasted?"

"Couldn't have been too many years," Krissy said, nestling back against him. She fit under his chin, in his arms, perfectly.

"Of course not," he agreed.

Only forty or so, Jax commed with a snort. *But it wasn't tapas I was eating there… Ah, the senoritas…*

He shrugged his disinterest and whirled Krissy around to face him, capturing her lips. Not for any reason, other than because he could. And because she tasted good. And she stirred something in him.

"Wine's open," Jax interrupted. "Unless you're not drinking, Krissy?"

"I'd love a glass. No work tomorrow."

"And no risk of regrets?" he murmured into her hair.

She looked up at him, clear-eyed. "None at all."

Gods, he was starving, his stomach rumbling, but it was all he could do not to pick her up and carry her through to the bedroom right now.

His lips paused in her hair. When she said she wanted to renegotiate the no P in the V…had she been hinting that she wanted him alone? Inside her?

Gods, why did he want her to mean that, when he *couldn't*?

Jax pulled his phone from the back pocket of his pants and shoved it across the counter. "Krissy, you might want to take a look at that, so we're all on the up-and-up."

She flushed a little as she scanned the medical report. "Actually, that's an expression I've never understood."

Jax grinned, ladling pasta into a tureen and covering it with a rich tomato and anchovy sauce. "On the up-and-up? Reckon Erik and I'll be able to show you a bit of that, soon as we've eaten."

She chuckled, a delightfully filthy sound. "I hope you're done with the cooking, then. Divine as it smells, I have other…hungers."

Erik cleared his throat, concentrating far too hard on pouring the red wine into goblets. He handed one to Krissy and shoved another across the steel bench toward Jax. Then raised his own. "To…?"

"Mutual satisfaction," Jax suggested.

"Living in the moment," Krissy said.

"Pleasure." That's all he'd ever chased. He needed nothing more.

Did he?

They ate sparingly, teasing and bantering, drawing the meal out, a prelude to what would follow. Delayed gratification always made for greater pleasure, but he'd never found the waiting so hard before.

As they finished the bottle of wine, he pushed from the table. Extended his hand to Krissy.

This was it. The culmination of his desire for her.

Yet right at that moment, he knew he was wrong. Sure, there'd be a hell of a finale, but *culmination* implied an ending.

Which wasn't about to happen.

But how could he tell her that?

Krissy rose into his embrace. She pressed close, her mouth opening to his. Jax moved behind her, undoing her shirt, letting her skirt fall to the floor.

She stepped free of the pile of material. Took his hand and Jax's and led them to the bedroom.

She pushed his shirt up, above his pecs, her lips on his chest, hands moving to his belt as he tugged the fabric free. He refused to read anything into the fact that she always seemed to face him. That she chose to undress him first. That she still hadn't allowed Jax to kiss her.

Boundaries? Jax commed.

He was tempted to set a whole lot Krissy hadn't mentioned. Instead, he kissed her, pretending he wasn't exulting in being the only one allowed to do so. "What do you want, Krissy?"

Her breath caught, her pupils dilated with lust. "Everything. I want *you* to show me. To teach me."

"Rules?"

She shook her head. "No rules. None. I want it all."

Her eyes flickered closed as Jax's hands covered her breasts, tugging her back to lean against him. Hands behind her, she struggled with his fly as he bit at her neck. "You say stop any time you change your mind, okay?" he said.

Eyes still closed, she nodded. Erik stepped back, admiring her naked body, wrapped only in his cousin's hands. Gods, Aphrodite couldn't have had a thing on her, despite his grandfather's stories. "I need to taste you, Krissy."

Her lips curved, and she parted her legs a little, the dampness of her sex catching the light. An arm wrapped around her waist to keep her in place, Jax kicked his own pants aside and then reached down, over her hips, to spread her open.

Erik plunged his tongue into her sweetness. Krissy groaned, arching farther back against Jax.

"Gods, Krissy, you're so damn sexy," his cousin murmured, comming an instant later, *dude, she's so fucking hot.*

Yeah, like he hadn't noticed.

"Erik." Her tone was breathy. "Don't make me come yet, okay?"

He grinned and nipped at her clit, grazing it with his teeth as Jax rolled her nipples between his thumb and finger. "But I want to taste your honey, honey."

She placed her hand on his head, pushing him away, trying to adopt a serious expression, though lust slackened her jaw and pouted her lips. "I want you inside me."

Fuuuck.

He'd known that was coming—but hearing it almost made him come.

Intervention? Jax commed.

He was tempted to ignore his cousin. Pretend he hadn't heard and plunge his cock inside Krissy's welcoming warmth.

And lose his immortality.

He nodded at Jax, who spun Krissy around. She gasped as Jax's cock rode the furrow of her labia.

And watching her tight ass gyrating was in no way helping his own self-control. Palming his cock, he stroked slowly, trying to desensitize himself as he shoved to his feet.

"Erik," she gasped. "I want you."

How the hell was he supposed to ignore that? He pressed behind her, his fingertips tracing through the sheen of sweat glittering across her shoulders as her backside undulated against his thighs. "How, Krissy? How do you want me?"

"You know how." She sounded desperate.

"P in the V?" He tried to swallow his chuckle.

Really? Jax snorted.

"Yes," she gasped.

"Is that all, Krissy?" Thing was, he couldn't give her that. Not without Jax's help. "Or do you want Jax inside you, as well? Do you want his cock in your ass, Krissy?"

"Yes! God, yes!"

Jax's equally enthusiastic agreement almost prevented him hearing her response.

Six strides took him to a wall panel opposite the chaise at the end of the bed. At a touch, the panel slid back to reveal a huge mirror.

He returned to the couple, wrapping his arms around Krissy, nuzzling her neck, wreathed in the fresh, sweet scent of delicate orange blossoms, as his cock probed at her ass. Gods, the dichotomy of her beauty and her filthiness tore him apart. He wanted to plunge his dick back inside her, yet he wanted to worship her. But he couldn't have everything.

Sit over there. Lube's under the seat, he directed Jax.

Krissy moaned, shifting her feet to give him access as the head of his cock nudged her tight bud. "Uh-uh. Not me. Not this time. P in the V, remember? I'm going to fuck your pussy, Krissy. But first, I'm going to watch you take Jax's cock."

Her lips parted, her chest rising raggedly as she leaned back against him.

"Krissy, do you want to watch, as well?"

Her eyes flashed open. "How?" she whispered, sounding both terrified and impossibly excited.

He took her hand and led her to the chaise, where Jax sat, fisting his cock, slick with coconut oil.

Krissy bit at her lip, her eyes darting from Jax's

dick to him.

He leaned close to murmur in her ear, "Don't worry, sweetheart, he's smaller than me."

She giggled, but her hand trembled in his. Jax reached for her, tugging her closer, restraining his erection with his hand as he guided her pert bottom into his lap so she faced the mirror.

She kept her eyes down, avoiding their reflection.

Erik knelt in front of her, parting her knees. "You are so gorgeous, sweetheart." He stroked along her slick cleft, then eased his finger inside her. Where he'd soon be.

Her eyelashes fanned long and dark on her cheeks as she moaned, leaning back against Jax, grinding her bottom down, and he could feel Jax's restraint, the tension of his held breath as he kept his cock in check. He grinned, wanting to prolong his cousin's suffering. He'd be rewarded soon enough.

Krissy's pussy glistened, and he dipped his tongue into her, lapping at her swollen clit, tasting and teasing, her sweet, salty juice tightening his balls unbearably. She quivered, her thighs trembling, her suctioning, cushiony walls gripping his finger, as though it was sufficient to fill her. "Erik—enough!"

The urge to make her come on his tongue was almost irresistible. But that wasn't what she wanted. Not this time.

He groaned, took one more greedy lick, savoring her virgin essence, then moved aside. *Okay.* He nodded at Jax. "Open your eyes, Krissy."

She did so reluctantly.

"Watch in the mirror."

Her eyes dragged up to her reflection, her cheeks

flushing deeper.

Jax placed his hands under her bottom, lifting her so his cock sprang free, then rubbed along her swollen pink slit as he lowered her back onto his thighs.

Erik bit back his jealousy, forcing his attention to the pleasure on Krissy's face as Jax lifted and lowered her, his cock coated with viscous juice. She shuddered each time he brushed against her clit, the tremors quaking her small breasts, the nipples begging for his mouth to soothe them.

"Stand up a little," Jax urged. As she planted her feet on the floor and lifted from his lap, he fisted his cock and notched it against her ass. "It's all yours, Krissy. Take what you want."

She was holding her breath now, gaze rapt on the mirror as she hesitantly moved against the rigidity of Jax's cock.

Even if he'd wanted to look away, he couldn't. Her lips parted, eyes huge, Krissy was the horniest thing he'd ever seen. Millimeter by millimeter, she lowered herself onto Jax's erection, her tight pucker stretching to accommodate him.

"You don't have to take it all," Jax murmured. He kept his fist around his cock so it wouldn't penetrate too deep. "Try moving up and down a little."

Krissy fumbled, trying to work out where to rest her hands, her thighs trembling as she supported herself.

Erik shifted between her legs again. He kissed her, running his fingers through her hair, feeling her gradually relax, though she didn't allow herself to sink any lower on Jax's cock. *Lean back,* he commed to his cousin. As Krissy responded to his caress, her tongue stealing into his mouth, he took her hands, guiding them behind her so they rested on Jax's abdomen. Gripping her calves, he lifted her legs and placed her feet flat on Jax's thighs. "Try that. Lean back against Jax."

Holy hell, the view was amazing. She was spread wide open, Jax's cock disappearing into the rosebud of her ass.

"Oh, yes," she gasped. "Oh, fuck, that feels good."

If the view had been a turn on, hearing her vocalize was near enough to tip him over the edge. He closed his eyes, trying to limit the sensory overload.

"Erik." Her voice was breathy.

"Enough, sweetheart?"

"No. I want you."

He'd never been so hard in his life.

Jax reclined farther, his muscles rippling with the effort of holding the angle, drawing Krissy back with him.

Erik leaned over her, wanting to kiss her but knowing she was having enough trouble breathing. "Both of us, Krissy? Can you take us both?"

She wound a hand around the back of his neck. Her other hand found his nipple ring, tugging him closer. "I want to," she whispered, almost as though she was asking him if it was possible.

He swallowed hard and grasped his cock, stroking it between her pouted lips, the silvery strings of her desire linking them.

She let go of his neck and stretched her hand to his butt, digging her nails in him. "Fuck me, Erik. I want you inside me."

Gods. That was all he wanted. All he could

remember ever having wanted.

His gaze glued to her face, he slowly sheathed his cock in her, every inch swallowed by her intimate, lush ripeness. She clenched around him, the tendons in her neck straining as he and Jax slid against each other through the thin membrane. Her eyes were closed, her breaths short and sharp. He couldn't tell how much was pain and how much lust.

But he knew how to get her off.

"Gods, Krissy, my cock's all the way inside you. My balls are pressed right into your hot, wet snatch. But I want more." She whimpered, and he leaned forward, sinking in even deeper, nipping at her earlobe as Jax's hands moved up over her breasts. "Krissy, you're going to make me come. I'm going to fuck my load all the way up inside you. I can't hold back."

As he'd suspected, proof of her own desirability was the key. Her eyes shot open, her muscles clenching him tight as the building orgasm rippled through her.

"Oh, fuck, yes," Jax grunted, his knuckles whitening on Krissy's breasts. "Fuck, yes, Krissy, you're gonna make me come, too. I'm coming in your ass."

"Oh, my God!" Krissy's knees pressed against his hips as she drove her groin toward him, her moans loud and unrestrained, the contractions squeezing his cock like a steel-ribbed sponge. "Oh, my God. Yes. Make me come. Fuck me!"

Chapter Twelve

His jaw darkened by overnight growth, black hair tumbled across his forehead, Erik looked younger asleep, more relaxed. Or perhaps just totally exhausted, like her. As he stirred, his long eyelashes flicking open and closed, he stroked a hand down her cheek. "Morning, sweetheart."

Lips pressed the nape of her neck, and Jax's hand, trapped beneath her as he spooned behind, cupped her breast, the other stroking her flank in long, firm, seductive sweeps.

It seemed inconceivable—yet unspeakably beautiful—that, desire temporarily slaked, she'd slept secure in the arms of these stunning men.

Erik shifted closer, his lips seeking hers, the embrace deepening as he hardened against her leg. His hand slid to her hip, pulling her close even as Jax's length probed her from behind. Both men were ready to go. Again.

And so was she.

Jax's hand slipped between her legs, stroking, caressing, making sure she was ready, as Erik's tongue delved into her mouth. She folded her fingers around his cock, and he thrust in her hand as Jax entered her from behind. A whimper escaped her lips. Even tender and exhausted, she'd never have enough of them.

"Come for us, Krissy," Erik said against her lips.

"Before you say a word, come for us."

She did.

And they did.

As Erik lifted his long leg from where he'd used it to pinion hers, she thrust half-upright. "What time is it?"

Jax toyed with her nipple. "Only six thirty. And Saturday, so I vote we spend the whole day in bed."

She shook her head, pushing off the loose sheet covering them, debating which ripped, muscular body to climb out over. Erik was the wrong choice; he seized her hips, settling her over his groin, half-erect again. "Just give me five seconds, sweetheart."

"No, we have to go. We have to get to town."

He pushed back the spill of dark hair from his face. "Don't need to be at the cop shop until eight. I let Trent know."

She scrambled out of bed, though she paused to lean forward to kiss him again, her nipples brushing the galleon on his chest. "No. The café. Trent will be there by seven. Along with Daniel and well, everybody else."

Jax sat up, the sheets bunched around his middle. "Dad? Am I missing something?" His biceps bulged as he reached up to secure his long blond hair with a strip of leather from around his wrist.

"You will be, if you don't hurry." She shot an apologetic glance at Erik. "I meant to tell you on the beach, last night. Before…" Maybe everything should be counted in orgasms. It could be her new thing. *I meant to tell you, five orgasms ago.*

Erik dropped his legs over the side of the bed, his shoulder muscles an ocean of undulations as he stretched. "Tell me now, sweetheart."

"Get dressed. I'll show you."

"Uh huh. I've played your 'show me' games before." He grinned sexily, prowling after her as she headed for the shower.

Gorgeous men should have to take far longer to get ready. To be fair, she did delay them somewhat, testing whether her memory of them all having fit in the shower together the previous night could be correct.

It was.

They did.

Still, both of the guys—*her guys*—were ready before she'd managed to tame her hair and given up on smoothing the wrinkles out of her blouse and sarong.

Jax held her panties up on one finger, his eyebrow lifted. "Looking for these?"

She huffed. "I have to go past home and get some fresh clothes."

"Are you sure we have to go out?" Erik pressed close, capturing her hips. "And if you are sure, are you *positive* you need underwear?"

She grinned and pushed him away with the heels of her hands. "Yes, and yes. Car. Now." She'd be turning up at The Little Blue with both men, and she didn't give a damn.

Christie wasn't home, and Seagull was very clear that he'd not been fed. Still, it only took her minutes to feed and pet him, then change into a long sarong and off-the-shoulder peasant blouse. Jax whistled appreciatively, and Erik dropped a kiss on her shoulder, taking her hand as they walked down the hill from her place to the main drag.

"What's going on here?" he said as they approached The Little Blue. Jax walked close on her other side. "I've only ever seen the place this busy for the surf carnival."

Excitement buzzed in her stomach at the sight of long trestle tables, laden with food, lining the alfresco dining area. So much more than she'd hoped for. "You know how I said I spoke with—"

"Krissy!" Adele's squeal interrupted as she darted toward them, clutching Daniel's hand. "What did you do? No, I mean, *how* did you do this?"

She couldn't hide her grin at Adele's evident pleasure. "It really wasn't me, Adele. All I did was speak with the other retailers along the strip. They were happy to come onboard."

"But…this?" Adele gestured toward the crowded tables, the chairs around them packed with customers. "I don't even understand what's going on."

"I guess you should consider it proof of how loved you are around here."

"Understandable." Daniel's deep burr hummed agreement.

She settled her bag on her shoulder, mostly because shifting it meant she could move a little closer to Erik. "The other vendors have agreed to close for business every Saturday morning until The Little Blue is up and running again. Obviously, that's not going to actually help you, so they've each also provided a dish or two, for you to sell." She pointed to the items she recognized. "Chia pots from Vegan Ventures. Bubble Tea from Bubbleish. Fruit salad platters and Bircher muesli from Beach Bites. Literally everyone chipped in. We made it a set-price, eat-what-you-like deal, so everyone tosses their money in the pot in the middle of the table and helps themselves. Oh, and because their businesses are closed, the traders are all here to buy their breakfast. No point having the goods without any customers."

Adele's throat bobbed, and she dashed a hand across her eyes. "I can't—I can't believe this. It's too much."

"How exactly did you persuade everyone to do this?"

Erik's murmur raised tingles along her neck. She was exhausted, yet the slightest attention from her men had her ready to go again. "Fundraising events are kind of my thing. That's largely what I do for Ocean Conservation. So this was a no-brainer."

"You're fully qualified, then." Christie stalked up behind her.

She turned, ready to spar with her sister, but Christie jerked her head. "I saved you seats over here. Thought maybe you'd be held up and get here late." She eyed the two men, then nodded. "Well done, sis. Way to break out of your weird rut."

"Who's calling who weird?"

"Least I'm not beige."

Despite her words, Christie's tone lacked some of her customary snark, and Krissy frowned as she followed her twin, trying to nail the reason.

Christie waved to three empty seats, then took one almost opposite, turning to speak to the couple alongside her, Elena and Tyson.

As Jax greeted his brother, Erik called down the table to Trent, who had his arm around the shoulders of a voluptuous woman. "Bro. Krissy, I think you know everyone except for Jayde, Trent's life-partner." For some reason, part of the table fell silent, as though the information held a deeper import than the words lent.

Jayde lifted a hand and smiled, flushing as the attention fixed on her.

"And Isaak," Erik said, "a recruit from the States."

"Ma'am," the lanky blond drawled.

"I'm going to find us coffee," Jax said as Erik reached across the table to the platters, piling food on all three of their plates.

"Dig in." Erik nudged his chin at her overloaded plate. "You need to keep your strength up."

"You mean we're not going back to bed after this early start?"

"I totally mean we're going back to bed. Soon as Trent and I've done the police station, we're off."

"Oh, you're going there, too?" She took a spoonful of wild berries and chia pudding.

Erik lifted one shoulder. "Won't hurt to look at the footage again. The more eyes on it, the better." He raised his voice. "Actually, Dan, Elena, guys. You should all come look at the tape. You get plenty of tourists up your way, never know when something might click."

Christie looked toward them as Erik spoke, watching him for a moment before her gaze shot to Daniel, assessing him. Then she turned, pushing her fingers through her thick, blonde hair and chatting animatedly with Elena.

Krissy frowned. There was definitely something going on with her twin.

Jax's hand landed on her thigh beneath the table. "Eat. Drink. Because we're sure going to be merry soon."

"What's with you guys and urging me to eat?"

Erik snorted into his coffee. "Guess we just love putting things in your mouth."

"Lucky I have an insatiable appetite, then."

Jax's hand tightened at her words, and she caught the quick rise of Erik's chest, the flare of his nostrils.

"Hey, Steve," Adele called from the end of the table. "Nice to see you here."

The sergeant nodded a general greeting as he approached. "Happy to help raise funds, 'Dele. Even happier to grab some breakfast." All the seats at the table taken, he reached between Elena and Christie for an empty plate. Elena took a plate for him and loaded it with food. Christie's lips pinched, signaling her annoyance at the interruption.

Krissy relaxed, sipping at her coffee. That was more the prickly sister she knew and occasionally loved.

"Thanks heaps." Steve took the plate, standing a little straighter and taller as he smiled at Elena. Hiding behind the rim of her coffee cup, Krissy glanced furtively left and right, relieved Jax and Erik were paying more attention to their food than to the exotic beauty. Kudos to Adele for not feeling threatened, but she'd be the only female at the table not imagining an unwinnable rivalry with the graceful woman. Well, except for Christie.

Steve waved his fork at Trent. "When you're done here, mate, can you come over to the office? We'll get that stuff out of the way, then I'm off crabbing for the weekend."

Trent pushed back from the table. "Do it now, if you like. Won't take a minute, then you can make the most of your time off."

"Sure. Hang on." Steve leaned across the table, closer to Elena this time. "'Scuse me." He snagged a croissant, despite having two on his plate already.

Krissy stifled a giggle at his obvious move, but Elena gave him a sad, yet devastatingly attractive smile. "If it's okay, Sergeant, a few of us would like to look at the footage. We're based at a lifeguard station farther north, so we see quite a number of tourists pass through."

"You're a lifeguard? Wow. I might take up surfing."

Christie snorted and pushed back her chair, which meant Steve had to shift away to let her up. Elena's gaze followed as Christie stalked from the table toward the bench holding the coffee machine.

Krissy frowned, her fork paused halfway to her mouth. Maybe she was imagining things?

"We'll just duck over to the cop shop," Erik interrupted her puzzlement. "Meet you back here?"

She shook her head. With only two days in a weekend, she planned to be near him as much as she could, soak up the enjoyment along with the sunshine.

Them. Near them, she meant.

Though, if she was honest with herself—which was what was supposed to happen now—while Jax was hot as hell and fun, it was Erik she gravitated toward. Erik she kissed. Erik whose lead she followed.

Maybe it was because he'd been first. Her first real lover.

And perhaps the reason why she felt this way didn't even matter; she simply needed to accept it as fact. Erik excited and intrigued her. He was sexy and raunchy. Filthy when she needed it. Demanding and compassionate. Kind. Thoughtful. In fact, everything she could want in a lover, able to fulfill her in every way.

Jax and the other lifeguards would leave soon, returning to their base farther north. And she and Erik would remain at The Bay. Which meant…exactly what did that mean? And why did her stupid heart leap with sudden hope, as though there was some possible future for the two of them together? As a couple?

She rolled her lips over her teeth, biting at them as she blinked furiously to banish the prickle of tears behind her eyes.

Because the immutable fact was that Erik had made it clear he was interested in a polyamorous relationship. She'd agreed to that—hell, she'd jumped at the chance—and she couldn't renege now. Didn't want to renege, because Jax was fun, a taboo experience she'd never forget. But when he left, she'd have no interest in including another man in their sexual fun.

Because she no longer needed to.

And because she wouldn't compromise for any man, that meant she'd lose Erik.

She tried to shake off her thoughts. Erik took her hand, his thumb massaging her knuckles as he chatted with Trent while they strolled the sun-splashed street toward the police station. Live in the moment, right? She had to be happy for what she had, not wish for what couldn't be.

Jax dropped back to speak with Tyson, and Christie sidled up to her, speaking so softly Krissy gestured for her to repeat the question.

"What do you know about Elena?" Christie

muttered.

"What do you want to know?" she teased, then regretted being mean as she followed her sister's gaze to the willowy beauty walking in front of them with Isaak. "Actually, nothing other than what you heard. She works up the coast with Jax and the others. They're going back week after next." The words punched her stomach. Ten more days with Jax was fine, but it also meant only ten more with Erik.

"Has she got anything going on with any of them?" Christie muttered.

"I'm sure they'd like there to be. Definitely not with Dan, that much I know."

Christie gazed straight forward. "Do you think you could find out? I mean, like, ask one of your guys?"

Her guys. Or her guy? Either way, yeah. She could do that.

Chapter Thirteen

He had firm hold of Krissy's hand as the Mer packed the tiny police station. Sometimes he forgot how large they all were. Even Elena, with her graceful proportions, was several inches taller than the average human and often kept her hands hidden, probably embarrassed by their proportionate size. Not at the moment, though. Several times he'd noticed her touch Christie's arm, their heads close together as they spoke, Christie occasionally giggling, though Elena was, as always, solemn. The women were probably rating Steve, given Elena had already dismissed all the Mer present.

Not that he cared anymore.

He had bigger problems.

Like finding a way to explain to Krissy that, just because he was willing to share her, it in no way detracted from how much he liked her.

Like *really* liked her.

Like couldn't-get-her-out-of-his-head liked her.

Like when-Jax-left-what-the-hell-was-he-going-to-do liked her.

Like maybe-immortality-wasn't-all-it-was-cracked-up-to-be liked her.

Like he-was-totally-fucked liked her.

Except he was being stupid, and he knew it. Lack of sleep, dehydration, overexertion, whatever. He'd get over it soon enough.

Then she nestled against him as the room crowded, flashing a smile up at him.

And he knew exactly why Trent had been willing to risk his life for Jayde.

Yup. He was so fucked.

When Jax left, she wouldn't want to know him. Not unless he found a third person to join their scene. And he didn't want to do that. Not anymore. He'd walk away rather than share her with anyone else.

Except, how could he?

His hand tightened on her waist, as though he could imprint her into his side, remember how she felt, how perfectly she melded against him.

Hells, how was he going to survive this?

There were too many broad shoulders for them all to fit in the smaller secondary office, so Steve carted the computer out and set it on the raised reception bench. Cued the tape. The Mer didn't need to see it to know what it contained; he'd already commed them. But only Trent would know if the barely discernible hulk lurking in the shadows of the mango trees was the same guy who'd attacked him.

That's him. The thought commed from Trent to all the Mer. "I've seen this guy around," he added for the humans.

Sudden anger surged through Erik, the muscles across his back tensing as he tried not to allow his fury to transmit to Krissy. It was thanks to this bastard he'd almost lost his brother.

"Where?" the sergeant asked.

"The marina, up the coast."

He's Mer? Isaak asked. *So why would he burn*

down the café if he's not one of the hipsters Erik laid into?

It's common knowledge The School hang out at The Little Blue, Trent commed. *He's sending another warning to the Mer to back off the illegal longliners he sold us out to. He's so deep in their damn pockets he'll never see daylight.*

He'll never fucking see daylight again if I get my hands on him. Erik bit down on his lip as Krissy glanced up at him, seeming aware of his anger, despite his silence.

Steve played the tape through again. "I'll take the print up to the marina on Monday, see if anyone can identify him. It's a long shot, though, with the poor picture quality. It'll be hard to get a conclusive ID."

"No, it won't." Elena's soft voice trembled. "I know him."

There was a rustle of interest in the room, drowned out by the battering of questions in his head, as all the Mer mentally turned toward Elena.

She closed her thoughts so they couldn't pry, but spoke aloud. "He's my ex." A shudder rippled through her, and she crossed her arms tight over her chest, looking away from the screen as though she couldn't bear to see the man frozen on there.

"This *guy*?" Christie blurted. "Shame."

Elena took a deep breath and turned to Christie, ignoring the others. "Among my…culture…there is a pressure to breed. Regardless of personal preferences. It is hard to break away from expectations."

Silence, both physical and mental, reigned in the room for only a second.

Ah, Tyson commed to him and Jax. *Well, at least I*

don't feel so bad about striking out now.

Christie laid her hand on Elena's arm. "Believe me, I know what you mean. Well, not so much about dickhead exes, that's more Krissy's thing. But about expectations."

Krissy tensed, and he pulled her closer, pressing a kiss into her hair. Her sister sure had a caustic tongue.

"Excellent," Steve said, then winced, realizing his poor choice of words. "That is, excellent on the ID, I mean. If you'd like to come through to the office, Elena, I'll take some details. Unfortunately, the footage doesn't evidence any wrongdoing, but it'll give CI a starting point for investigations."

As Elena went into the rear office, Christie following her, the rest of them trooped out into the bright sunshine.

They walked toward The Little Blue in near silence, though the Mer commed frantically between themselves, and Daniel and Adele talked quietly.

Jax, Tyson, and Isaak paused to offer far-too-much help to a pair of female tourists who were wrestling a flat bike tire, and Erik seized his opportunity, drawing Krissy away from the group, through the swaying trees on the foreshore, and down the slope toward the beach.

To their spot.

To where it had started.

To where he was willing to end it.

She grinned up at him as she slipped off her shoes and burrowed her toes into the golden warmth. "You're determined to indoctrinate me into actually liking this sand stuff, huh?"

He stripped off his shirt and dropped it on top of her shoes, the sun mellow and smooth against his skin.

"I'm working on breaking down your aversion toward fantasies of all sorts."

"Mission accomplished." She leaned into him, stretching to put a hand around the back of his neck, drawing his lips down to hers.

Unusual nerves pulsed in his throat. Could he tell her? Though, for the first time, the secret of the Mer seemed less important than the other secret he kept from her. The secret of his desire. "You know, there's more than one kind of fantasy that could become reality."

She sniggered. "Maybe we need to save some for another day. I'm pretty knackered."

"Dirty girl."

She glanced up at him through her eyelashes, suddenly hesitant, her soft cheeks sunset pink. "Actually, I'm kind of serious." She chewed at her lips for a moment. "Though maybe I can find a little more energy…because it's nice to have just you, for a change. If you know what I mean."

She may as well have reached into his chest and yanked his heart out. Laid it bare and bleeding in front of them. If wanting her was going to hurt this bad forever, what kind of curse was immortality?

"Just me? No Jax?"

The hand she'd laid on his chest trembled as she traced his tattoo. "Maybe not always Jax."

"You have someone else in mind?" His voice came out rougher than he planned, and he sucked in a jerky breath, as though that'd help him control his tone.

She shook her head but dropped her chin so he couldn't see her eyes. "No. I thought…maybe sometimes it could be just us?"

Gods, surely it wasn't his own desire speaking? There was no way for him to misinterpret what she said. Was there?

He kissed her cheek, the side of her mouth, her lips as his mind whirled. She was asking for commitment. For monogamy. And unknowingly, for him to sacrifice immortality.

Yet even as he tried to chase the thought, to be logical and rational, he lost himself in the taste of her as she unstintingly gave back everything he offered.

As he eventually raised his head, he sucked in a deep breath, his fingers working beneath her blouse. "Just us, huh?"

She nodded, and he tilted her chin up to look at him so he could read her eyes. "Krissy, are you talking about monogamy? I know how you like rules, so let's get it out there."

She bit at her lip again, and he pressed a brief kiss to soothe the reddened flesh before she spoke. "I...well, maybe. After Jax leaves. I thought we could...try it out...? I don't want to—" She broke off, then spoke in a rush. "I'm sorry, but I lied about the Sunday papers, okay? I, like, really get off on reading them. Especially the real estate pages. And turmeric lattes rock."

He couldn't hide his grin. "Well, to be fair, I kind of led you astray, too."

She cocked her eyebrow, and he tugged her closer, taking a moment to nuzzle the side of her neck.

"I like when you lead me astray," she murmured.

"Mmm. But the thing is, when I was talking about fantasy becoming reality, I didn't mean the physical kind. Not this time." His heart pounded against her palm, the galleon tossing in a stormy sea. Shit, could he do this?

How could he not do it?

"Feels pretty physical to me." She leaned in against the erection that had become a permanent part of his anatomy.

He licked his lips and took one of his last breaths as a Mer. "I meant more the fairies and unicorns and…mermen kind of fantasy. I have a story to tell you." If Elena was courageous enough to speak her truth in front of Mer and humans alike, he should be brave enough to live his truth.

He wasn't jealous. Jax was welcome to share Krissy, for as long as *she* wanted.

But there was one more first he intended to claim for himself.

A first for him, at any rate.

He wanted to make love with this woman who had stolen his heart.

Whatever the cost.

Chapter Fourteen

Though Erik accepted her sudden reversal regarding monogamy, he appeared more serious than she'd ever seen him, despite his crazy talk about fantasies becoming reality.

Maybe he was leading up to having a dig about her tirade when they'd met, where she'd insisted that love was nothing but a ridiculous fantasy.

Back then, it had been a fantasy.

Several days ago.

Or using her new counting methodology, about a dozen orgasms ago. A slightly aching heart ago.

Because that was the truth of the matter; Erik made her heart ache.

And impossibly, it wasn't the debilitating, incapacitating pain she'd feared love would bring. Instead, the ache created a conscious awareness of what she might be capable of, the emotions she could allow. Maybe even enjoy.

A longing to know whether Erik felt the same way surged within her, and she blew a quick breath between pursed lips. She had to take the risk. "I know changing my mind must sound stupid—"

Erik quirked an eyebrow. "Stupider than unicorns?"

"You're being unfair to them. I'm sure they're intelligent, really. Like horses." Heavy with the perfume of ripe mangos, the breeze drifted Erik's hair across his eyes. She slid her fingers through the short fade and wound them into the silky length. A feeling of…connection…pulsed through her hand, and despite her nerves, Erik's calm reassurance throbbed though her.

"They're more like donkeys, I promise you," he said.

A tiny smile tilted the corner of his lips, and she pressed it firmly into place with a kiss. "You know a lot of unicorns, then?"

"Obviously not a *lot*. They tend to keep to themselves. Probably because, like us, they were hunted for centuries."

Her hand slid from his head, though she left it on his chest, registering his elevated heartbeat. "Like us? You mean, like people?" She screwed up her nose, gazing at him. His hands had shifted to her hips, holding her close, and the contact wasn't helping her think. "When you're around, I'm pretty sure my brain doesn't work properly. I'm having trouble following this conversation."

He flashed her a grin. "That's definitely a case of my fault, not yours. Look, Krissy, what I've got to tell you is going to sound crazy." His forehead furrowed as he turned from her to stare across the calm ocean. Then he ran a hand through his hair and shook his head. "There's no way to make it sound less than nuts. I guess that's why I've never told anyone before." He shot her a long glance. "Well, that and because I've never cared enough about anyone to tell them before." He took her hand, his thumb caressing her palm. "Which is just a whole other level of crazy, but"—he lifted one shoulder—"can't help the way I feel."

If her heart swelled any more, it'd burst. Whatever it was he wanted to tell her, one thing was clear; he felt the same way about her as she did about him.

She laced her fingers through his. "Okay, let's do crazy together, then. Spill."

His lips found hers, and somehow he tasted of the salt of the ocean, fresh and clean. His tongue caressed hers, and he drew back reluctantly. "It'll be easier if I show you."

Her hip pressed to his groin, she smiled. "I'm always up for you showing me…"

"Come for a swim with me."

She cringed. The ocean was undeniably beautiful, but the hidden dangers in the unknown depths terrified her. "We just ate. Aren't we supposed to wait a while? Like, preferably, about three hours? Or could we just wade in the shallows?"

Erik's fingers played under her shirt, tracing delicious trails across her skin. "I'm a lifeguard, remember? I'm not going to let anything happen to you."

"You'll show me all the safe ways to get wet, right?" she teased. "But also, there are sharks out there. After that breakfast, I'd be a three-course meal for even the slowest."

The laughter dropped from Erik's face. "If I promise I'll never let anything bad happen to you in the ocean, will you trust me?"

Of course she shouldn't. He couldn't make that kind of promise. Yet right then, as he towered over her, his huge body exuding strength and security, she couldn't imagine any harm ever befalling her. "Is this swimming gig just an excuse to get my clothes off? Because I'm all in, if that's the case."

His fingertips traced the underside of her breasts. "Considering the time of day, we probably should act with a little more decorum. Though if you're offering, I doubt I'll ever be able to refuse you…"

"Oh, I'm offering, all right." She quickly stripped to her panties, delight coursing her at the instant narrowing of Erik's eyes, the flare of his nostrils.

"Nice move. Now, purely for the sake of decency, I *have* to get in the water." He grinned, drawing her toward where the sea curled in gentle waves against the sand.

The velvety water caressed her calves, then her thighs, as Erik guided her deeper. He turned to face her, the current stroking them.

"Krissy, those fantasies I mentioned?"

She slid her hands up his forearms, the muscles cording beneath her palms. "The ocean seems to have been a good place for sharing them, so far."

He nodded, his jaw tense and throat working. "God, I hope so." He tilted his head toward the water swirling between them. "Look."

Like before, beneath the water, his skin shimmered with an odd iridescence, the light shifting and moving so it was hard for her to focus, or pinpoint a source of the illumination.

She peered at her own skin through the crystal water. "How is it you get the body glitter, but I don't?"

Erik dipped his hand into the ocean and brought it out dripping, then traced a path down her chest, between her breasts. The droplets sparkled and glistened with an otherworldly luminescence, a thrilled rash of goosebumps chasing them across her skin, although the air was balmy.

Erik's darkly shaded jaw worked, his frown deepening as his forefinger tracked across the slight swell of her breast to circle her nipple, leaving a sparkling trail. "The thing is, all the stories you grew up with…fairies and elves and unicorns and…mermaids? Well, they're not so much fantasies as history."

She snorted, though her nipple had painfully doubled in size at his touch. "Uh huh. You're trying to tell me they're all real?"

He traced a design on her chest with one finger. "Of course they're not all real. That'd be ridiculous." He lifted his hand, and she gasped as the image of a heart sparkled upon her skin. "But they are based in fact. The same way that myths are based in legend. You humans try to explain things you don't understand by pretending they're nothing but stories."

"*You* humans?" Her stomach lurched and contracted. No. This wasn't fair. He was so perfect; there couldn't be anything wrong with him.

He'd been joking about being nuts.

Hadn't he?

The wash of the ocean was suddenly loud in her ears, drowning the pounding of her heart.

Erik's gaze held hers, his tone measured, as though he implored her to understand. "I totally know how this sounds, Krissy. There's no easy way to put it, but—" He shifted his hand between them and flicked his wrist. A membrane appeared between his fingers, refracting the sun in rainbow arcs and sparkling with the same iridescence as his skin.

"No," she whispered.

Yet that wasn't what she meant.

Because this revelation, this physical proof of his difference, made Erik beyond perfect.

Despite the yearning of her heart, despite her intention to enjoy life to the fullest, to take Adele's advice and live in the moment, still she'd had reservations about her ability to give her love to a man.

But Erik clearly was not a man.

She closed her eyes for a second, fighting the dizzying unreality of the situation, trying to ground herself, to force herself to think rationally.

But she didn't want to. She wanted to allow her heart to soar, she wanted to squeal in delight, and she wanted to fall into Erik's arms.

When she flicked her eyes open again, Erik still stood before her, his forehead furrowed, his fists clenched, carefully not touching her. Waiting for permission, as he always did.

She tentatively placed her hand over his heart, almost expecting to feel something unusual.

Nothing, except the firm, steady beat beneath the taut muscles. She nodded, licking her lips and trying to find her voice. "So. Not human. What, then?"

Surprise flickered across his face. "Mer. I guess you'd be more familiar with the concept of mermaids, though."

Her hand drifted across his pecs, and she grinned. "You sure don't feel like I'd expect a mermaid to. So…Mer?"

His hands still fisted, he gazed at her warily. "That's it."

"And that means what? Besides the fact that you sparkle like a vampire."

He snorted. "They don't sparkle; that was a well-executed PR exercise. Being Mer means I swim well and can hold my breath for a ridiculously long time."

"So going down is no challenge?" She pointed into the water.

He grinned at her innuendo. "More a passion."

"That's potentially a very acceptable superhuman ability. Other than that, you're, well, human?" She shook her head slightly. The situation was ludicrous, yet she felt perfectly calm.

"Mostly. With a couple of anomalies."

Her gaze ran over his muscled torso. "There don't seem to be any superfluous body parts, or notable exceptions." As he'd still made no move to touch her, she closed the distance between them, her hands sliding around his back, making her intention clear.

The tension in his shoulders eased, and his palms grazed her shoulders, then swooped down her back and over the curve of her butt as he tugged her closer. "You don't think this Mer thing is going to be a problem?"

She lifted one shoulder, her nipple brushing his chest. "Why would it be? So we're different races. Australia prides itself of being multicultural, right?"

His deep voice thrilled through her as he bent to capture her lips. "Krissy, you are the sexiest, most amazing woman. But I have to tell you everything, before we go any further."

She nodded, but it truly didn't matter what else he felt obliged to explain. Her heart finally understood what her body had known from the instant she first saw him on the beach.

Erik was the one.

Epilogue

Seagull skittered around Krissy's feet, though the kitten's interest was really in grumpy old Midge. He dashed toward the blind cat, feigning an attack, but pulled up a few inches short, then padded forward and gently nuzzled her.

The ancient cat purred, batting her head into his side and grooming the scruffy juvenile with a rasping tongue.

Within two hours of arrival, the pair had forged a firm bond. Now, a week later, it seemed Midge had a new lease on life, devoted to caring for the orphan.

"I know it's predictable, but the combination of tongue and pussy is giving me ideas," Erik murmured in her ear as he settled his arms around her waist.

She leaned back, his warm breath stroking her neck. As though this Mer-man could ever be predictable. "Interesting. I thought you'd had years to hone your ideas, not to mention, your fantasies. I didn't realize you were reliant on outside stimulation."

"I'll give you outside stimulation," he snorted. His hands ran up beneath her loose shirt to cup her breasts, thumb and forefinger rolling her nipples.

Heat instantly centered in her loins, but she pulled one of his hands free, caressing his palm as she brought it closer to her face.

He kissed her ear, low laughter thrumming through

him. "Again?"

"Always again. Every time you ask that, for whatever reason."

"Insatiable woman," he groaned, but shook his wrist to release the beautiful rainbow webbing between his fingers.

She ran a finger across the iridescent membrane. How was it possible that this gorgeous man—no, given his heritage, not to mention his looks, he was more god than man—how was it possible he wanted her so badly he was prepared to give up everything to be with her?

"Never gets old, huh?" Erik murmured.

She winced at his choice of words. Because now he'd had sex with her, without Jax present, he would get old.

He'd sacrificed immortality for love.

And while that scared her, the depth of her own feelings for him did not. The thought of sharing whatever time they had left thrilled her.

But the delight was tinged with sadness; Erik was older than he looked. Like, decades older. No, centuries older. And he didn't know how long it would take for the Mer curse to catch up with them. It didn't seem to have affected Jayde and Trent yet. But Jayde was part-Mer, and that wasn't the case for her. She could only hope that whatever physiological changes loving a Mer brought about in a human, they'd take her before she lost Erik.

She kissed Erik's fingertips, forcing away her melancholy.

Live in the moment, as Adele had said.

"Peacocking, are we?" Entering the room through the arched doorway opposite them, Jax nodded at Erik's fanned hand. He spread his own fingers, his webbing shot through with darker blues and purples than his cousin's. "If that display is all it takes to win a beautiful woman, I would've tried it years ago."

"Maybe takes a little more than that, cousin," Erik's deep voice burred, the stubble of his jaw grazing her temple. "But it's worth everything."

Jax nodded, unusually serious. "It'd take a lot to persuade me of that. And maybe you've stolen the one woman who'd have been able." The corners of his eyes creased as he strode across the room, taking Krissy's hands in his strong grip.

Sandwiched between the two men, the familiar flare of desire kindled in her loins. Erik had her heart, but that would never mean Jax didn't have access to certain other places.

Jax's hand went around the back of her neck as he pressed his lips to hers, his tongue seeking, tangling with hers in a kiss that was both erotic and a farewell. He drew back slowly. "So you think Erik will be enough for you now, Krissy?"

The erection pressed hard against her backside was sufficient evidence to make her smile. "I think we'll do fine. Besides, you're coming back when the Senior Council next meet, right?"

"Then, and I suspect I may be visiting far more often than I previously have." He grinned.

Erik's hands roamed over her breasts, his chin on her shoulder. "And you'll always be welcome," he said, though his voice held a note of caution. "But remember to check with Krissy first."

Jax's gaze met Erik's above her head. "I hear you, man. Consent, right?"

She felt Erik nod. "Every time."

"Okay." Jax tugged her against his narrow hips, the delightful friction of his hard on and Erik's teasing her. "I guess we've had our 'one last fling' three times now. I really should be going. Let you two get on with your perusing of the Sunday papers, or whatever it is boring old couples do together, right?"

Somehow, she doubted that a single minute alone with Erik would be boring.

Jax extended his hand and grasped Erik's forearm, the muscles rippling. "Catch you in a few weeks, then."

They moved to the front door to watch him leave, striding toward the bluff, where crashing waves sent spume high into the air. Though she'd seen both Erik and Jax dive from there, heading out to the mysteries of The Cavern, deep in the ocean, still nerves climbed her throat each time she watched one of their beautiful bodies arc high into the heavens before plummeting down.

Erik's lips nuzzled her ear, and he turned her toward him, nudging the door closed with one foot.

She ran her hands up over his naked chest, tracing the ship sailing across his pecs, then the mermaid on his arm. "Oh!" She snatched her hand back. "I just realized. You said this tattoo was of your mother. You were actually serious, right?"

He snorted. "Nope. Be a bit weird to have a picture of Mum on my arm, wouldn't it?"

"Better not be an old girlfriend, then." She narrowed her eyes deliberately. With over two-hundred years of experience, Erik had more exes than she'd ever be able to deal with. But it didn't matter. He was hers now.

His fingers traced her jaw as he gazed down at her. "Krissy, what Jax said. Do you think I can be enough for you now?"

She smiled, pressing her palm against his cheek. "Jax is that once-every-so-often indulgence. You're my main course. You're enough for me, Erik. Now, and forever."

However long that would be.

Laney Kaye

About the Author

A professional counselor by trade and author of young adult, contemporary, and women's fiction under her "real" name, Laney Kaye writes hot merman and shifter romances, perfect for a quick read to spice up your day…or night!

~*~

Visit Laney at
https://laney-kaye-author.weebly.com/
Twitter:
https://twitter.com/LaneyKaye1
Instagram:
http://www.instagram.com/laney_kaye_author
BookBub:
https://www.bookbub.com/profile/laney-kaye

~*~

To chat with Laney Kaye and other Wild Rose Press authors of erotic romance, join us at
www.groups.yahoo.com/group/thewilderroses.

Hook

The Lure of the Mer Book One

By Laney Kaye

Marine biologist, Jayde Collins, has a love affair with the ocean. Lucky for her, because lately, swimming is the only way she can get wet without investing heavily in rechargeable batteries. While out diving, she's caught by the crew of a trawler, beaten, and dumped as shark bait. Rescued and magically healed by a hot lifeguard, she's not sure if she's dreaming, but with the erotic fantasy he offers—sex with two men—she's not sure she wants to wake up.

Trent Okeanós leads an elite group of Australian lifeguards who hide a secret; they are the last of the Mer. His law forbids sex with humans unless another Mer joins them, but when he saves Jayde, he's unprepared for the jealousy warring within him. Yet if he dares let his lust turn to love, Jayde will be bonded to him for life and he'll be stripped of immortality.

Lovers by Midnight

Monster Ball

By Ashantay Peters

Hexed by two witches in 1805, the ghostly Lt. Jonathan Tempest has been celibate for over two hundred years. To break the curse, he must attend the coveted Monster Ball and seduce his reincarnated fiancée by midnight or suffer a grim fate. But these witches don't play fair, and with a mumbled incantation, his odds of making a connection plummet. He now resembles a human frog. Good thing costumes are encouraged.

Bethany Julian isn't looking for a happily ever after with a prince. All she wants is a one-night stand at the Monster Ball. Sick of being mistreated by handsome men, she chooses a man who is kind rather than hot. But there's more to the lieutenant than meets the eye, and she finds herself swept off her feet—and into his arms.

Chased by security and demons and threatened by witches, Tempest and Beth are on the run as the clock ticks. Only time will tell if their physical attraction can break the curse forever...

Thank you for purchasing
this publication of The Wild Rose Press, Inc.

For questions or more
information contact us at
info@thewildrosepress.com.

The Wild Rose Press, Inc.
www.thewilderroses.com

To visit with authors of
The Wild Rose Press, Inc.
join our yahoo loop at
http://groups.yahoo.com/group/thewildrosepress/